Philippa Fisher

and the
Fairy Godsister

Philippa Fisher

and the
Fairy Godsister

Liz Kessler
illustrated by Katie May

CANDLEWICK PRESS

For my brother, Peter,
who I hope won't mind having a book
about fairies dedicated to him;

and for Fiz,
to make up for not being around for
every step of the journey this time

Text copyright © 2008 by Liz Kessler
Illustrations copyright © 2008 by Katie May

Second U.S. paperback edition 2015

Library of Congress Catalog Card Number 2008933678
ISBN 978-0-7636-4070-5 (hardcover)
ISBN 978-0-7636-4596-0 (first paperback edition)
ISBN 978-0-7636-7462-5 (second paperback edition)

14 15 16 17 18 19 BVG 10 9 8 7 6 5 4 3 2 1

Printed in Berryville, VA, U.S.A.

This book was typeset in Hightower and Maiandra.

Candlewick Press
99 Dover Street
Somerville, Massachusetts 02144

visit us at www.candlewick.com

Contents

Can I see another's woe

And not be in sorrow too?

Can I see another's grief

And not seek for kind relief?

No, no! never can it be!

Never, never can it be!

— William Blake
from "On Another's Sorrow"

ATC

"So who's next on the list?"

"I thought we could try this one."

"For 3WD? Are you sure? She hasn't worked directly with humans before."

"We've all got to start somewhere."

"Granted, but she does have particularly strong feelings about them. You know how she took the incident last year with her friend."

"That was a high-risk assignment. He was a bumblebee, for clouds' sake!"

"But still . . ."

"It'll be fine. We'll give her a flower life cycle—a nice, gentle way for her to make contact. All she'll need to do is position herself perfectly, and she'll be picked with love and care and admiration. No danger of being swatted!"

"You're sure she's ready for this?"

"It's time she started on the extra tasks. She needs to start deepening her compassion. She'll have to if she's ever going to move on."

"We'll need to monitor the assignment closely."

"Ray will cover it. He's supervised her before."

"Well . . . OK. It looks like you've got everything covered. Let's do it."

"Good. I'll tell 3WD that we're ready to go."

chapter one
TREE HOUSE

Sunday morning began with the awful realization that I'd made the biggest mistake of my life.

It had all started on Saturday. The weekend began like any other. Mom and Dad were rushing around, packing puppets and balloons and face paints into the van for a party in the afternoon. There's nearly always one going on somewhere on Saturdays. They're party entertainers; the weekends are their busiest time. I used to go along to the parties, but then I — well, I just don't anymore.

Birthdays, anniversaries, passing your piano exam — anything you want to celebrate, they'll be there, singing, pulling rabbits out of hats, throwing pies at your big brother. Whatever it takes to make you smile.

Other kids think it must be great to have them as my parents. They think my home life must be a nonstop party. Um, not quite.

It used to be fun, I suppose — when I was young enough not to get bored with making dogs out of balloons every week; when I actually liked being driven around in a bright yellow VW van with pictures of clowns and jesters and rabbits on the side; when I didn't know that there was any such thing as a problem that couldn't be sorted out with tickle therapy. I used to think that my parents were the most incredible human beings on the planet.

Now I just think they're embarrassing.

This Saturday I didn't mind, though. I hardly even noticed them. I was busy putting the final touches on a present that I was making for my best friend, Charlotte.

"Philippa, we're going now!" Mom called up the stairs.

"OK," I shouted back.

"There's tofu rolls and veggie burgers for you and Charlotte."

I rolled my eyes. Once, just once, it might be nice to have something normal, like grilled cheese or fish fingers, for lunch.

"Great!" I replied, hoping I sounded more sincere than I felt.

I looked up as my bedroom door opened. It was Dad. He had a bright orange sun painted on one cheek and a black night sky with a crescent moon on the other.

"Which hand's the penny in?" he asked, grinning widely as he held his palms out.

I pointed to the penny in his left hand. "That one."

"Are you sure?" Dad winked. Then he closed his hands, shook them, got me to blow on them, and then — presto — the penny had disappeared. It was a good trick. It was probably even better if you hadn't already seen it approximately three times a week for eleven and a half years, and if you didn't already know how to do it yourself.

Still, I'd never say anything. It would only upset him, and I did secretly enjoy his magic. I liked it when he showed me how to do a new trick. I'd go away and practice it for days afterward. Not that I'd ever do it in front of anyone except Charlotte.

Just the thought of performing made me tremble. I'd *never* do that again.

"Neat," I said, smiling.

Closing his hands again, Dad reached forward, tickled my ear, and opened his palms. "Hey, look where I found it! It was in your ear the whole time," he said. "Now, why didn't you tell me?"

I kept smiling. "They'll love you, Dad," I said.

He leaned over to kiss the top of my head. "Be good, sunshine," he said before leaving me and bounding downstairs to join Mom.

I watched the van drive to the end of the road, and then I got back to the friendship bracelet I was making for Charlotte.

Charlotte had been my best friend since the first day of school. We had even been in preschool together, so we'd known each other for nearly seven years — and this weekend she was moving away. Her parents had bought a farm hundreds of miles away. They were "getting back to nature." All homegrown food and solar panels and no phone or TV. They weren't even going to have a computer, and it was so completely in the middle of nowhere that they probably wouldn't even have cell phone reception. They might as well have been leaving the planet.

They were really excited about going, though. Even Charlotte. All I knew was that it felt as if someone were about to chop off one of my limbs. That's how close we were. Charlotte said she felt the same way, but I knew she was looking forward to her new life, too. She was going to have a pony of her own, and her parents said they'd get a dog and chickens. I was happy for her. Really, I was. But how was I ever going to be happy without her around?

The friendship bracelet! She'd be here any minute. I wiped my eyes and got back to work. It was a really complicated pattern in turquoise, pink, and purple: all her favorite colors.

I'd just threaded the last piece of cotton into place when the doorbell rang. *That's the last time she'll walk over to my house*, a heavy voice said in my mind.

I looked in the mirror, wiped my eyes again, and practiced smiling. *Don't think about it. Don't let her see how sad you are; don't make it hard for her*, I said to my reflection.

*   *   *

"I want to say good-bye to the tree house," Charlotte said as we ambled through the backyard. The tree house was "our" place. We'd shared so many secrets and games there. The tree house knew everything about our lives.

Dad had built it when I was a baby. He said it was a labor of love because of something that had happened a long time ago. Years before I was born, my dad was traveling, when he realized that he'd run out of money and had nowhere to sleep. He met an old man begging on a street corner. Dad felt bad that he couldn't give the man any money, so instead he emptied out his bag and told him to take anything he needed. The beggar took an apple from Dad, and they got into a conversation.

When Dad told him that he had nowhere to sleep, the man mentioned a place on a nearby beach where there were huts built on stilts. Dad set off for the huts, and that's where he met Mom. She was working in the area for the summer. He ended up staying for three months and got a job there, too. Then they spent the next six months traveling together. They were married almost as soon as they got back.

He'd modeled our tree house on those huts.

The tree house is right in the middle of a clearing at the far end of the backyard. It's huge and round and built on top of three tall wooden legs, with a wooden roof that looks like a giant umbrella. It's got three great big windows in the sides and a ladder that takes you into the hut through a trapdoor in the floor. If *we* ever moved, I'd miss the tree house more than the house.

You could easily fit five or six people in there. Usually it's just me and Charlotte, though. Mom and Dad don't bother with it nowadays, which I'm glad about, because there's so much of my stuff in there. I don't think I'd want anyone prowling around! It's full of private things, like my diaries, and notebooks filled with ideas for stories and lines of plays that Charlotte and I have started writing together, and letters and notes that we've left there for each other.

It's also littered with cards and newspapers from the magic tricks I practice on Charlotte. I probably do them really badly and look stupid, but when I'm doing a trick, it's like nothing else exists. Charlotte's always so nice about watching them. Her favorite is the one where I make a coin disappear and then get her to peel open an orange and the coin is inside the orange. It's so easy, but she's never guessed how I do it. She tells me everything I do is brilliant. But that's a best friend's job, isn't it?

I won't have anyone to tell me I'm brilliant after she moves.

"You coming up?" Charlotte called from the top of the ladder.

"I'll wait for you here. I thought it'd be nice for you to say good-bye on your own," I said. The truth was that it would probably make me cry if I had to listen to her say good-bye to our special place. Charlotte looked at me for a second, then she just nodded and climbed into the tree house.

I sat down in the clearing to wait for her. The sun had been trying to come out from behind the clouds all morning. Now it was trapped behind the biggest lumpy white cloud in the sky. As I watched, the cloud narrowed and lengthened, stretching into a new shape. The sun started boring holes through it, dusty bright rays poking out through the gaps. When that happens, I always think it looks like cosmic staircases coming down from heaven or from another planet, and that if we could only find a way to climb them, we'd be able to discover a whole new world that existed right beside ours.

I once told Charlotte what I thought, and she laughed and explained in great detail why it was scientifically impossible. She says I don't need other worlds anyway, because I live in a dreamworld of my own half the time.

I must get it from Mom. She believes all sorts of crazy things like that. She reckons that sun rays are fairies coming down to visit the world and look after all the humans. She used to sing a song to me that she said would make fairies appear. We'd sing it together sometimes.

Fairy come, fairy go,
Fairy, oh, I need you so.
If I count from nought to nine,
At midnight, fairy, please be mine.

We sang it every day for about a year and never saw a single fairy, so I eventually decided that it was just a silly song she'd made up—even if she did try to convince me she'd learned it directly from the fairies themselves!

I leaned back on my hands, singing the song to myself and letting the sun warm my face as it gradually broke free from the cloud, edging out so brightly that I had to turn my face away.

As I looked down, I noticed a clump of daisies beside me. I picked a couple of them, slicing the stem of one and pushing the other through it.

Charlotte's shadow fell over me. "What are you doing?" she asked, sitting down next to me.

"Making a daisy chain."

"Cool. I'll join you. I haven't made one of those in ages," she said, picking a couple of daisies of her own.

We worked in silence for a while, each lost in her own thoughts. Were hers the same as mine?

Was she as sad as I was, or was she too busy being excited about going to live on a farm and having a pony of her own?

The thoughts made my eyelids sting. I turned away from Charlotte and concentrated on looking at my daisy chain. I counted up the daisies. Eight. Almost enough. One more should finish it off. I was going to make it into a necklace and give it to Charlotte with the friendship bracelet.

The last daisy is always the hardest one to find. It's got to be long enough to fit the head of a daisy through the stem, and strong enough to stay in one piece and hold the whole necklace together.

The trouble was that the daisies were all looking a bit blurry through my tear-filled eyes, so it was hard to know which one to pick. I quickly brushed the back of my hand across my eyes and continued the search for the perfect daisy.

As I stared, a breeze blew across the clearing, making the daisies dance and sway. One of them stood out instantly. It was taller than the others and seemed to bend right over, toward me, almost as if it were asking to be picked. I reached out for it. As I did, a tear plopped out of my eye, landing on the daisy.

"Oops, sorry," I said absentmindedly. The daisy nodded back at me, as though accepting my apology.

It had understood me! The daisy had heard me; it had answered me!

I turned to Charlotte, about to tell her, but then I remembered how she responded to the sunbeam-staircase theory and a hundred other ideas I've had over the years that she's pointed out are physical impossibilities. She'd only say the same about my daisy. And on this occasion I supposed she'd be right. Even I had to admit that flowers don't talk!

Turning back to the daisy, I reached carefully down to the bottom of the stalk and pulled it out of the ground. As I did, the strangest feeling came over me. A kind of sparkling inside. That's the only way I can describe it. There was a buzzing sensation, starting in my fingertips, then spreading up my arms and into my body, filling me with an itchy tingle. I squirmed and wriggled as I took a closer look at the daisy.

Looking down at it in my palm, a thought filled my head. No, it was more than a thought. It was a kind of knowledge, almost a certainty. The daisy was a . . . No—it couldn't be. I was being ridiculous! It was probably just because I'd been thinking about Mom's silly song. I could still hear it over and over again in my head.

If I count from nought to nine . . .

That daisy had been the ninth one I needed for the chain!

That was when I knew it was true—even if it sounded crazy, I absolutely knew it.

At midnight, fairy, please be mine.

The daisy was going to turn into a fairy at midnight.

I need to get one thing straight before I go any further, in case you're like Charlotte and concerned with what's sensible and logical.

I don't actually believe in fairies.

Or I didn't. I mean, I—look, I'm eleven and a half years old, not a little kid. I'm in middle school now! I *can't* believe in fairies!

If someone had asked me last week if I did, I'd have said definitely not . . . I think.

I certainly wouldn't have thought there might be one living in my backyard!

But something deep inside me told me that there was. And you'll just have to trust me on this for now, OK?

I peeked at Charlotte to see if she had read my thoughts. Her tongue was poking out at the edge of her mouth as she concentrated on her daisy chain.

"Just got to get something from the tree house," I said. Charlotte nodded without looking up.

Closing my palm gently around my daisy, I crept up the ladder and searched around for something suitable to put it in. Rummaging through the old magazines and puzzle books, I found it. A small, oblong, copper-colored tin with a picture of an oak tree on its lid. Mom had bought it for me in a gift shop when we were on vacation last year.

I'd been waiting for something special to put in the tin. And now I'd found it.

I grabbed a bit of dry grass that was lying around on the tree-house floor and pressed it into the tin. I know it sounds stupid, but I wanted to make sure the fairy would be comfortable. Then I put the daisy into the tin and placed it carefully on the window ledge. There isn't actually any glass in the windows; they're just big gaps in the walls with chunky wooden ledges. "See you later," I whispered to the tin, feeling a bit silly. Then I climbed back down the ladder to join Charlotte.

"Done!" she said, brushing her legs as she stood up. I quickly found another daisy and completed my chain.

"It's for you," Charlotte said, holding her daisy chain out toward me.

"Mine's for you!" I said, smiling as I held it out to her.

Charlotte smiled back. "Let's make sure we keep them forever," she said.

"Forever and ever!"

I slipped my new necklace over my head, trying to tell myself that the daisies wouldn't wither and die, and that our friendship wouldn't either.

"Come on, I've got another present for you," I said. "It's in the house."

Charlotte followed me, and we chatted about lunch, presents, the weather, flowers, parties — everything we could think of, except the thing that was bigger than all the others put together: the fact that she was leaving tomorrow.

I went to bed early. Mom and Dad always let me stay up late on Saturdays, but I didn't want to. I didn't want to watch them come back all giddy and excited, like they usually do after they've done a party. I think it's all the sweets they eat. They play music really loud and dance around in the kitchen. Mom sometimes plays her fiddle, and Dad does a silly jig.

I used to dance with them. Occasionally, I still do — when they won't take no for an answer — but to be honest, I never feel comfortable dancing around in the kitchen. Sometimes I try to get out of it by saying that I need to do my homework. That makes Mom hoot with laughter. Homework is *way* down on her list of priorities, compared with such important things as dancing and laughing.

They didn't push me tonight, though. Maybe they could see I was too miserable. Charlotte was leaving in the morning. She wanted me to see her off, but I couldn't face the thought of watching her drive out of my life.

I checked the clock radio on my nightstand. Ten

minutes to nine. This time tomorrow she'd be in her new home.

Then I remembered something else: the daisy! I almost laughed out loud as I remembered thinking that it was going to turn into a fairy. That's what having a mom like mine does for you: it gives you strange ideas! Fairies — as if!

But there was still a bit of me that wondered if perhaps it could be possible. My head filled with questions. I mean, what if it *was* true? What if it really *was* going to turn into a fairy?

What would she be like? Would she like the tin I'd made for her? What if she grew out of it?

Maybe she'd have a wand that sparkled, and a bright white dress, and a tiara in her hair — she'd look like all the fairies you read about in stories. Stories I used to read *ages* ago, that is. I don't read those kinds of stories anymore — of course!

I laughed to myself. I couldn't persuade myself I was going to have a real, live fairy in my yard!

I picked up a new magic book that Dad had bought me last week: *The Magician's Handbook.* I opened it to a new trick: "How to Make Paper Clips Link Themselves."

But after staring at the words for ten minutes, I

realized I hadn't turned the page. In fact, I hadn't even read a line. I couldn't get the daisy out of my mind.

What if . . . ? What if . . . ?

I couldn't stop wondering. Maybe I just wanted to believe it to take my mind off of everything else. I don't know. All I knew was that the thought wouldn't go away — and the certainty was getting stronger and stronger.

I was getting jittery. Should I go down to the tree house and look at the tin, see if anything had happened yet? Would I disturb the fairy if I did? How did it work, anyway — the process of a daisy turning into a fairy?

I tried to go back to my book but still couldn't concentrate on it. That was a first. Reading about a new trick usually got my thoughts away from everything, whether it was thinking about Mom and Dad embarrassing me in front of my friends, or girls like Trisha Miles at school picking on me and making me look stupid in front of the class. Or even the thought of Charlotte going away. Magic tricks could usually take my mind off of anything. Not this, though. Maybe fairy magic was even more powerful than human magic.

I got out of bed and wandered around my bedroom, feeling clumsy and heavy. What could I do? How was I going to get through the next three hours? Should I go to the tree house? Should I just check?

I thought about the tin on the ledge, the darkness starting to grow around it. What if she was lonely or scared? My fairy, all alone, waiting in her little tin box on the window ledge. What if she came early? What if she'd left by the time I went to see her? What if she woke up—or came to, or whatever it is they do—before she was meant to? She might not be fully formed.

A shiver snatched the back of my neck, twisting hairs into spikes and tiptoeing down my spine.

Don't think about it.

I looked at the clock again. It was nearly ten. Only two hours. I got back into bed, grabbed *The Magician's Handbook*, and tried to read, wondering if the next two hours would ever pass.

Eventually, I drifted into a restless sleep.

I was being chased by a monster. It had short, thick legs like tree stumps, and branches sticking out of its head. It was coming after me with a bunch of daisies, shouting angrily as it ran: "You should have left them alone, you stupid child. Now look what you've done!"

I hid behind an oak tree. Could I climb it? It was surrounded by a beautiful daisy chain, but when I reached out, the chain turned to barbed wire. I was trapped, the monster was closing in on me —

"N-o-o-o!"

I jerked up in bed, sweating and shaking and even more convinced about the daisy. The dream — it had felt so real.

I blinked and squinted in the semidarkness. The light from the moon was shining through the curtains. It threw a menacing line of light onto the wall and carpet. I switched on the lamp and sent the moon away.

Twenty to twelve.

My mind was suddenly racing with questions again, like a carousel that wouldn't stop. What if she was a bad fairy? What if she didn't want to be in my tree house?

Maybe it was mean to put her in a tin.

Maybe she'd be mad at me already.

I got out of bed and pulled on my robe. I drew it around me, but I still couldn't stop shaking. Ten to twelve. *Think. What should I do?*

Eight minutes to twelve. Seven, six.

I couldn't do it. I didn't want it to happen.

I didn't want fairy magic. Why was this happening to me? Why did I have to make that stupid daisy chain? The shaking turned into a full body rattle as I realized I had to get rid of the daisy.

I darted out of my room and ran downstairs, making sure to avoid all the creaky floorboards near Mom and Dad's room. Gently turning the key in the back door, I ran as fast as I could down to the tree house, my feet damp from dewy grass.

Breathless, I clambered up the ladder, into the tree house, and across to the ledge.

"I'm sorry," I whispered, picking up the tin. "I'm really sorry."

I carried it to the opposite window, the one that looked down on bushes and shrubs. I opened the tin and then, leaning out the window, I scrunched the daisy tightly in my palm and threw it out, out into the bushes, away from the tree house, out of my hands, out of my life.

Moments later, I sagged with relief as I heard the distant church bell chime twelve times. Hands shaking, I stared at the empty tin.

As an afterthought, I threw that out into the

bushes, too, before climbing back down the ladder and shutting the trapdoor behind me. Without turning to look at the bushes, I ran up the lawn, back in the house, and straight back to bed.

Pulling the duvet up to my chin, I turned to the wall and somehow drifted off into a peaceful sleep.

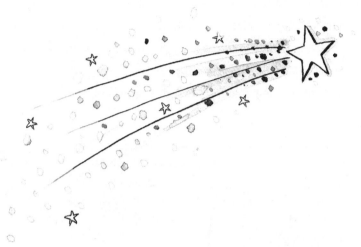

The first thing I noticed when I came around was the taste in my mouth. What was it?

Something gritty, unpleasant. I reached up to feel my mouth. It was all over my lips. Soil! *Ugh!*

I spat it out and wiped my mouth with both hands. *Argh!* My right arm! It was scratched and bleeding all the way down—and it hurt like mad. Was it broken?

I tried to move but couldn't put the weight down on my right leg. My ankle had swollen up. I could hardly see anything in the pitch blackness. Where was I? My head was fuzzy with confusion and unanswered questions.

I dragged myself out of the bush, scratching my back on thistles and prickles on the way. Glancing around to check that no one had seen me, I scurried over the fence into the woods. I washed the blood and soil off myself in a stream, smarting from the cold against my raw skin. What had happened? Was it always like this?

I sat on the bank and waited for morning to come.

chapter two
MOVING DAY

Bright daylight crept into my bedroom, searching out the gap in the curtains and seeping through it to aim straight at my face as if it were a target.

I rubbed my eyes and pulled the duvet over my face. Surely it couldn't be morning yet?

Lying under the covers as my brain gradually surfaced from the fog of sleep, for a moment it felt like any other morning. Then one by one, memories of the previous day entered my mind, each one weighing down heavier than the last.

Charlotte's moving today. That was the first. That was bad enough. I tore my mind away from the thought, and it instantly grabbed another one.

The daisy.

My heart hurt as though it had a giant snake wrapped around it, squeezing it tightly. My daisy. What had I done? My one and only chance to have a fairy of my own, and I'd thrown it away.

I dragged myself out of bed. The daisy chain Charlotte had given me lay on my dresser. It was starting to wilt already, and one of the daisies had come loose.

"I'm not going to lose you on top of everything else," I said, glancing around for something to put it in. This daisy chain represented my friendship with Charlotte. I wasn't about to let it die before she'd even left!

I scrabbled around in the cupboard under my dresser and found a small eggcup with a swirly green pattern around the top, and purple and blue spots all around the sides. I'd won it in the egg-and-spoon race at Easter. That would do. I filled it with water from the glass on my bedside table and put the stray daisy in it. It seemed to perk up right away. "That's better," I said, and went downstairs.

Mom was in the kitchen, sewing up a hole in a child-size policeman's outfit while she drank a cup of coffee. Mom works in a costume shop in the afternoons, as well as running the business with Dad, so seeing her fixing a policeman's outfit over coffee wasn't as unusual as it might sound.

"How come you're up?" I asked. Mom and Dad don't normally get up before me. I'm nearly always awake first, followed by Mom, who usually gets up while I'm fixing myself some breakfast — or what passes for breakfast in our house. Sugar-free, additive-free, taste-free muesli that most people would give to their pet rabbit, or organic rye toast that's a bit like eating thinly sliced bricks.

Mom gets all our food from this shop called Leaven Heaven, where everything is organic and fair trade — and generally lacking in taste, flavor, and chewability. Breakfast at our house is not the most exciting event in the world.

Mom spends most of the morning drinking coffee and shuffling around in her nightgown. Dad gets up and throws some clothes on just in time to bundle himself into the van and drive me to school. You wouldn't exactly call either of them morning people.

"Had to fix this outfit. We've got a little boy coming in to pick it up today for a birthday party,"

Mom said. "Anyway, I couldn't sleep," she added, draining her cup and getting up to refill it.

"How come?"

"Oh, one thing and another. Your dad woke me in the middle of the night, saying he heard noises."

"Noises?" Had he heard me creeping out of the house in the night? Was I going to be in trouble? Not that Mom and Dad are big on punishments. Or discipline. Or school. My parents are what you could call free spirits. They go with the flow and don't get too bothered by the kinds of things most people's parents get worked up about.

I hardly ever get into trouble anyway; it's not really my thing. But on the odd occasions when I accidentally do something I shouldn't have, all that happens is that we sit around the kitchen table and talk about it. Sometimes that makes me *want* to do something really bad, just to find out how they'd react.

"I think he's finally losing his marbles — what he's got left of them," Mom said with a laugh. "Said he thought he heard things going on in the backyard."

"Really?" I said quickly, crossing the kitchen and

opening the fridge so I could hide my burning face. "What time?"

"Well, the first time he woke up was at midnight."

"Mm-hm," I said as casually as I could. Here we go. We'll be having one of those discussions later. I'll have to look them both in the eye and explain why I left the house in the middle of the night, and they'll look at me with those sorrowful expressions that say, *Where did we go wrong?* Honestly, why can't they just ground me like *normal* parents?

"But it went on much later than that. At least for an hour, he said."

"Huh?" But I was back in bed by ten past midnight!

"Yes, he said he heard this noise out back. Not that I heard anything. Mind you, I could sleep through a bomb going off. Remember that time in —"

"What did he hear, Mom?" I burst in before she was off on one of her tangents. Honestly, Mom takes forever to tell a story. She gets sidetracked so many times that she usually forgets where she started.

"Now, don't say anything, because it might have been the wine he had before we went to bed. You

know he's not a big drinker, but the party yesterday went so well, and —"

"Mom!"

"Sorry. Well, he said he saw bright lights, and
there was a kind of crackling noise. A bit like
static electricity, he said, or lightning. He got out
of bed to see what it was, and the strange thing
was, he said it looked as though it was coming
from our yard! Bright lights and crackling, popping
sounds."

"What did he do?"

"He woke me up and dragged me over to the window, but it had stopped by the time I was awake
enough to open my eyes. I said it was probably the
Hendersons next door."

"Maybe they were having a fireworks display,"
I said, relieved that that was all it was, and not
that they'd seen me running around in the middle of
the night. It wouldn't exactly be easy to explain.

"That's what I said. He wasn't convinced,
though. He was positive it was in our yard, or in
the woods out back. I'm sure he'll agree with us
once he gets up, though. Things make much more
sense in the morning, don't they?"

Do they? Did things make more sense to me this

morning than they had last night? As far as I could see, things made less sense today than they'd ever made before in my life. I'd thrown away an opportunity to have real magic, and my best friend was leaving. What made sense about that?

I stared at the cereal box as I ate, reading the words on the side till I couldn't see them anymore through my blurry eyes.

I arrived at Charlotte's panting and hot, my pulse racing.

Charlotte was just coming out of the house with a huge box in her hands. "You came!" she said. "I thought you weren't going to!"

I grinned. "How could I not?"

Charlotte's dad stepped down from the cabin of the enormous moving van parked in the road. It was the length of two houses. Big, white, and solid, it held their whole lives inside it.

"Come to help?" Mr. Simmons said with a smile.

"Um, I can if you want. I was just going to say good-bye."

"Only teasing, don't worry. We're all done now, anyway."

Charlotte put the box inside the van and came

back to me. "I'm just going to check my bedroom one last time," she said. "Want to come with me?"

"Sure."

Charlotte's bedroom looked to me like the skin of an animal that used to be full of life but was now empty and hollow. I didn't like it. We'd shared almost as many secrets in here as we'd shared in the tree house.

There was one last secret I had to share.

"Charlotte, something amazing happened last night," I said. "And something awful."

I told her about finding the daisy, about how I was so convinced of what it was, about what I did at midnight, and about how I felt this morning when I realized what I'd thrown away.

When I finished talking, Charlotte stared at me. Then she burst out laughing.

"What?" I asked, trying to smile with her. Had I missed something? What was the joke?

"You. You're so funny," Charlotte said. "I'm going to miss you so much!"

"I'm not being funny! I'm not joking. Charlotte, it's real. It's terrible!"

Charlotte peered into my eyes, then laughed again. "Come on, Philippa, you know it can't be real. It's not logical; it's not scientific. It's the kind of thing we used to make up years ago, maybe. No one believes in fairies anymore!

I met Charlotte's eyes, and as I did, my certainty about the fairy began to slip away. In fact, the more I thought about it, the more I felt stupid and ashamed. I mean, how old was I? What was I thinking? Charlotte was right. The daisy was just a daisy. There were no such things as fairies! I'd just wanted to convince myself that something special might happen to take my mind off what was really going on this weekend.

"It was nice of you, though," Charlotte said.

"What?"

"Making up a story like that, just for me. To make me laugh, keep me from feeling sad. You always think of others. That's why you're so great!"

I swallowed down my silly shame. Charlotte didn't need to know that I'd believed it. I mean, I hadn't *really* believed it, anyway. Not really. Only for a few minutes, maybe.

"Anything for my best friend," I said in as cheery a voice as I could muster.

"Charlotte, we're off!" Mrs. Simmons called up to us.

"We'd better go," Charlotte said, looking around her empty room one last time before closing the door behind us.

"Thanks for coming," Charlotte said. Then she hugged me and stepped up into the van. The three of them sat in the front together, Mr. Simmons driving, Mrs. Simmons with two big maps on her knee.

I just smiled. I didn't trust my voice to get past the stone lodged in the middle of my throat.

Charlotte pulled the door closed behind her, and I stood on my own outside her empty house, waving and waving and waving as the huge white van carried my best friend and all her belongings away to start her new life.

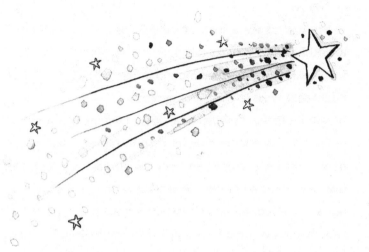

I stood in the glade, waiting for the pre-assignment meeting to start. *Come on, where are you?* Dawn, they'd said.

I glanced at my watch, noticing the stupid clothes I was wearing. They'd been left for me near the stream. I told myself it wouldn't be for long. But why did they have to put me in this department? I mean—*humans*!

I looked longingly down at the rushing water, sprinkled with sunlight in sparkly patches. My throat was parched.

I knelt down at the edge of the stream and scooped a few handfuls into my mouth. Much better.

What would I have to do to be a river one day? Or even a bird, or a squirrel, or a mouse? Did they have to work with humans, too?

"Daisy."

I turned to see a shaft of sunlight beaming down from a cloud all the way to the floor of the glade in front of me. Specks of dust flicked around inside it. The light was so bright that I had to shield my eyes.

"About time," I said, getting up and wiping my mouth.

I should have known better than to talk like that to my boss—but I was angry. And besides, it was only Ray. He was one of the soft ones. I'd worked with him a couple of times in the Seasons and Colors Department.

Some of them made you call them by their full names. FGSunray63728 was the worst. Most people called him by his nickname, the Godfather, but not to his face. Ray was the best of the bunch—which meant it was perhaps a little bit too easy for me to lose my temper with him. Not smart. I could still get into trouble with him—or get passed on to *his* superiors, the rainbows.

The sunlight flickered and danced on the ground. "Sorry to keep you waiting," he said.

"Just LOOK at me!" I burst out before I could stop myself. I was too angry—I'd deal with the consequences another time. I pulled up a sleeve to reveal a giant bruise spreading up my arm in a mottled mass of purple, black, and blue.

Ray's face glimmered inside the sunlight.

"We were all extremely sorry to hear of what happened," he said. "But you know that there's nothing we can—"

"And this!" I pulled down a white sock and stuck my left leg out in front of him. Specks of dusty sunlight spread and wavered in the air as he leaned forward to take a closer look at my ankle. I noticed him wince at the swelling.

"I could have broken them both!"

"We do take this seriously," Ray said gently, "and I've reported it back to the whole 3WD team. But the assignment has to go ahead as planned."

"But—but it can't!" I sputtered, limping around to make sure he could see how badly injured I was. "I never wanted to work with humans in the first place. You know how upset I was when my friend was swatted—before he'd even started his assignment! I told you humans don't care about us. They're dangerous and mean and callous. But you said it would be all right. You said that being a flower would be straightforward. And then she did *this* to me!"

"What would you like us to do?" Ray asked.

"I want you to take me off the case," I snapped. "Surely you can't expect me to work under these conditions!"

A sudden breeze brushed through the trees, shaking the leaves on an old willow.

"I can't do that," said Ray. "Once the drop of sadness has fallen on you, the assignment has begun. You were carefully chosen for this task. We need you to follow it through."

"Can't you do *anything*?" I asked, aware that my voice was coming out in a whine. I hated myself for pleading like that, but I hated *her* even more. "Couldn't you at least delay the start or something while I get over my injuries?"

"One moment," Ray said. He disappeared as a big fluffy cloud moved across him. I pulled back my sleeve and pointedly examined the bruises on my arm while I waited.

The cloud moved on and Ray was back. "I'm sorry," he said. "There's nothing we can do. Delaying the start will only cause problems. Now that you've been picked, you're on the life cycle. We can't risk you running out of time. Especially with this being your first fully solo assignment. You understand, don't you, Daisy?"

I nodded. I understood, all right. I had less than two weeks, if I was careful—or my life was at stake. Every assignment is a matter of life and death for fairy godmothers; we all understood that right from the start. You had to do the job within your life cycle, or the life cycle ended—literally. Under normal circumstances, there was always plenty of time, so it shouldn't have been an issue. But these didn't feel anything like normal circumstances to me.

"Come on, then," I said. "Give me what I need, and let's

get on with it." I reached into the sunlight and waited for the envelope and MagiCell to materialize.

"Good luck," Ray said as he faded away, glinting briefly across the trees and throwing a final spotlight onto the stream.

"Yeah, whatever," I replied. Then I turned and limped away.

chapter three

NEW GIRL

The first thing I noticed on Monday morning was the gap where Charlotte should have been. It was everywhere. First we drove past her house and didn't pick her up. I tried not to look at the empty dark windows and the SOLD sign on the lawn.

Next was crossing the playground all on my own. No one to complain to about my totally embarrassing dad, who always insists on dropping me off at school in the van. He can sometimes look a little crazy in the morning, grinning and waving till I get to the front door, his hair sticking out at every angle. Not that I can talk. At best, I could describe my hair as light brown and wavy.

In reality, it's mousy and frizzy and no matter what I do with it, it looks like a well-used mop.

Dad always gives me a great big bear hug before I can get out of the van, which I pray every morning that no one notices. You'd think he wasn't going to see me again for a month, the way he carries on.

And then he always has to toot the ridiculous horn as he leaves.

He had this special horn installed that plays the chorus to the Hokey Pokey. One time, when he was in an even better mood than usual, he actually got out of the van and did some of the actions. That was possibly the lowest point of my whole life. It got around the whole school, and for an entire semester kids would walk past me spinning around in a circle, sticking their left leg out, and then bursting out laughing. Yes, very funny. Very original. *You* try having my parents.

Dad always sits and waits in the van for me to wave at the gate before he leaves. So there's no way of pretending that I don't know him. The worst thing is when Trisha Miles arrives at the same time as me. She always makes some barbed comment. Usually I just grab Charlotte and run inside. I had no one to grab today, though, so I just gave Dad a wave and scurried in as quickly as I could.

Inside school, it was just as bad. I noticed Charlotte's bare cubby. And her seat next to me was empty, like everything else.

I tried to join in the general buzz as everyone came in, talking in high-pitched voices about what they'd all been up to over spring break. Lauren and Beth tried to include me. They sat at the same table as Charlotte and me. They're best friends, like us. I could tell they only really wanted to talk to each other, though, as they kept referring to things they'd done together and then laughing like hyenas.

They kept trying to explain the jokes, but I told them it was OK. I said I had things to do. To be honest, I don't always get their jokes, anyway. They're both into sci-fi and number puzzles, and they do things like write notes to each other in codes that no one else can understand. It was nice of them to try to include me, though.

I made myself look busy, opening the drawer under my desk to tidy it. There wasn't really anything to tidy, so I just moved my pens and pencils around a bit, and then pretended to be looking for something in my bag. At least I didn't have to worry about anyone trying to include me in their conversations or looking sorry for me.

"Is this seat taken?" a strange voice said.

I looked up to see an unfamiliar girl standing beside me. She had blond hair that framed her head in a curly mop. Her face was pale, but with pink splotches on her cheeks and bright green eyes that were staring into mine.

"I *said*, is this seat taken?" she repeated, pointing at the chair next to me. Charlotte's chair. A couple of the others nearby had turned to look at the new girl.

"I — well, no, I guess not," I said.

"Good." The girl pulled the chair out. She had a bag over her shoulder that squelched against her back as she sat down.

"Um, don't you want to take your bag off?" I said hesitantly.

"What? Oh, this. Yes, I was about to," she said snootily, dropping it on the floor beside her. Then she turned away from me and sat high in her seat, her back as straight as a wall. She drummed her fingers on the desk and looked sharply around the room, her lips pursed and eyes wide as she took in her surroundings.

A couple of the boys at the next table were staring at her with blank faces. The two girls opposite them were staring at her, too, only slightly more subtly. One of them smiled. The girl didn't seem to notice any of them.

Who *was* she?

I'd find out soon enough. She wasn't showing any signs of wanting to talk to me, so I decided not to ask.

Miss Holdsworth came in a few minutes later, and the room gradually hushed. "Good morning, 6B," she said, smiling at us all.

"Good morning, Miss Holdsworth. Good morning, everyone," we replied, as we did every morning. The girl next to me looked startled for a moment, then nodded to herself as though she'd just learned something new, and repeated what we'd said.

Most of the class looked over to see who'd spoken at the wrong time. A few of them laughed. I wanted to tell her not to worry; it didn't matter. Some of them laughed at you over anything. You got used to it. Kind of.

But she didn't look bothered. She still had that aloof look in her eyes, as if she were slightly above the rest of us, slightly removed.

"I see our new girl is here," Miss Holdsworth said, putting on her glasses and opening her attendance book. "Daisy, isn't it?" she said, scribbling away. "I haven't been given your surname yet."

"Surname?" the girl said.

"Your last name, dear," Miss Holdsworth said. She often called us "dear" when she was in a good mood. She was a bit old-fashioned like that. She was pretty strict as well. She called us all sorts of other things when we were in trouble. Sometimes they were funny. Lizzie Andrews once got called a fishwife for talking too much. We all laughed at that. We usually knew by the look on Miss Holdsworth's face when it was time to stop laughing, too.

Daisy glanced quickly around. Her eyes seemed to fall on the books I'd piled up at the edge of the desk. Then she snapped her eyes away and said briskly, "French. Daisy French."

Miss Holdsworth continued talking while she wrote Daisy's name in the register. "Philippa, you'll look after Daisy for her first week," she said. "Make sure you show her around the whole school. I don't want her getting lost." She looked up. "Is that all right with you, Philippa?"

"Yes, Miss Holdsworth," I said. I peeked at Daisy to smile at her, but she didn't return my look. She must have been really nervous. I wasn't surprised that she'd clammed up. I would have, too. I hate being put on the spot like that. I'd probably have turned bright pink as well. In fact, I could feel my cheeks burning now, knowing I was the center of attention, even if it was only for a few seconds.

While Miss Holdsworth took attendance, I kept trying to catch Daisy's eye to let her know I'd take care of her. It might take my mind off Charlotte not being here. Give me something useful to do.

As I glanced at her, I noticed she had a scratch on her cheek. Her arm looked bruised, too. I couldn't help wondering what had happened. Maybe she'd been in an accident. Perhaps that was why she'd had to start at a new school so late in the year. I'd look after her. I leaned over to whisper to her. "You'll be fine with me," I said.

Daisy turned to look at me. "I'll be fine *anyway*," she replied in a sharp whisper.

I felt as though I'd been slapped. My cheeks burned again.

I tried to tell myself that people act differently when they're shy. I'd still be nice to her. I'd still show her around. Apart from anything else, I'd be in trouble with Miss Holdsworth if I didn't.

We had P.E. first thing. It was a sunny day, and we were playing kickball. I noticed Daisy had quite a bad limp as we went outside. She went up to talk to Miss Holdsworth and must have gotten excused from playing, because she sat on the side for the whole game.

I was made an outfielder with one of the boys. I

hate that. You have to be good at catching people out, and catching is not one of my strong points. In fact, sports in general are a weak spot for me. I'm not terrible at them. I just don't have much coordination.

Trisha Miles was on the opposite team and high-fived her teammates every time I failed to catch the ball. I could see Daisy out of the corner of my eye. She rolled her eyes a couple of times when I missed the ball. She and Trisha looked like they were sharing a laugh one time when I fell over trying to catch it. Why didn't she go off and sit with Trisha, then? I didn't *ask* to take care of her!

I'd been jealous of Trisha's gang for years. They might be mean, but they were supercool, too; they were the ones *everyone* wanted to hang out with. I'd never gotten anywhere close. And here was some new girl exchanging knowing smiles with her, five minutes after arriving.

But Daisy hardly watched the game. Just sat there with her sweater on, fiddling around in her bag. It was so warm out, she must have been boiling. Why didn't she take her sweater off? At one point, she took something out of her bag. It looked like a cell phone. Good thing Miss Holdsworth didn't see. She'd have hit the roof! Daisy just sat there playing with it. She didn't strike me as someone who worried about what people thought of her.

"This is the cafeteria," I said lamely, holding the door open for Daisy.

As we stood in line, I mulled over the strange morning I'd had. The lunch line had that empty feeling about it, like everything else. Charlotte's absence seemed to be everywhere. The only things that took my mind off her were having to look after Daisy and wondering why she seemed to have such a problem with me. Not that either of those was much fun to think about.

Daisy picked at her lunch. I don't think she ate a single thing—just drank two cups of water. A group from our class crowded around our table, clearly wanting to check out the new girl. Daisy didn't even seem to notice them.

"I'll see you outside," she said, getting up after a few minutes of sitting together.

"You hardly touched your food."

"Not hungry," she said with a shrug. Then she drained a third cup of water and left me to polish off my lunch as quickly as I could.

She was leaning against the wall when I came out of the cafeteria. I tried smiling at her again. She just raised her eyebrows and started walking. I wanted to ask what I'd done. I mean, how could I have done *anything*? I'd never *met* her before this morning!

Whatever her problem was, it couldn't be anything to do with me.

We walked along in silence. Every time I opened my mouth to speak, I stopped myself and shut it again. I didn't want to give her an excuse to snap at me. With every silent second, I felt more miserable and missed Charlotte even more.

This was starting to feel like the worst week of my life.

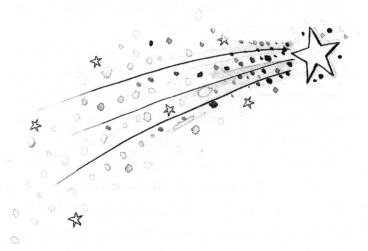

Why, why, *why*? WHY did I have to put up with this? Why couldn't they have taken me off the assignment? Why did they have to put me on it in the first place? They knew how I feel about humans. I was perfectly happy working on Seasons and Colors.

Anyway, I was here now. There was nothing I could do about it other than get the job done. And like it or not, I was responsible for Philippa—even if she thought it was the other way around!

I reached into my bag, thinking now was as good a time as any to get started. "I've got something for you," I said. I still wasn't sure how to get the assignment going without giving myself away. Why hadn't I concentrated properly during my training?

Philippa looked shocked that I'd spoken to her. Then she smiled gratefully. For a second, I almost felt sorry for her. Then I shook my head. *Humans hurt fairy godmothers without a thought*, I reminded myself. *They swat them, stand on them, and squelch them. They throw them out windows!*

I stopped feeling sorry for her pretty quickly after that.

I was about to pull the vouchers out of my bag when a couple of girls from our class came toward us. It was the girl named Trisha, with someone else. Now *these* were the kind of girls I could get along with. Trisha had a look in her eyes that I liked. A kind of sparkle. *So* much more fun than Philippa. Why couldn't I have been given her instead? It was obvious that her friends were the ones worth knowing around here.

Trisha and the other girl looked us both slowly up and down as they passed. *Hey, don't associate me with her!* I wanted to shout. *I'm only doing my job. I'm way different from her! Look at me—it's obvious!*

I couldn't say anything, though. I had to swallow my real feelings and put up with it. *Just get on with the assignment*, I told myself. *Get it done and get out of here.*

The girls passed us, laughing and whispering.

"Don't worry about them," Philippa said. "They're like

that with everyone. They think they're better than the rest of us."

Maybe that's because they are, I thought. "OK," I said.

I reached for the vouchers again, but as I did, my MagiCell started beeping in my pocket. "'Scuse me a sec," I said. Then I turned away from Philippa and checked out the screen. OBSTRUCTION TEN SECONDS, it read.

I breathed out heavily as I shoved the MagiCell back in my pocket. This was the bit that annoyed me most about having to work with humans. In training it was fun, but in real life—well, the thought of having to look out for her welfare all the time was making me mad. What about *my* welfare?

I pursed my lips to stop myself from screaming with frustration. Then, just as we got to the end of the corridor, I gave Philippa a quick shove. She fell against the wall. It didn't hurt or anything. I didn't push her hard, but she looked at me with shock on her face.

"What was that for?" she asked, her voice all pinched up and squeaky as if she were going to cry.

"Sorry—accident," I said simply, as a man rounded the corner carrying three large boxes piled in front of him so high that he could hardly see.

"Whoops, just missed you there," he said cheerily. "Good job. Full of paint, these boxes. That could have been nasty!"

As he passed, Philippa stared at me. She didn't say anything. Her mouth opened, then she shook her head and
tried a shaky smile. "Well, that was lucky—I guess I should
thank you!" she said.

"Yes," I replied tightly. "You should."

With that, I walked off, even more annoyed than before.
The afternoon bell was about to ring, and I hadn't given
her the vouchers yet. This assignment was not going as
planned!

chapter four
TRANSFORMATION

Wait!" I ran to catch up to Daisy.

"What?" she said without turning around.

"That," I said. "I mean—I know it sounds stupid, but it was almost as if . . ." As if what? My words trailed away. What was I trying to say, anyway? Whatever thoughts were going around in my head, they didn't add up. It certainly wasn't a good idea to say them out loud!

Daisy walked faster.

"But you couldn't have," I continued, my words slipping out before I could stop them. "I mean—I mean, how could you? You couldn't have known, could you? It's impossible."

Daisy rolled her eyes.

"But you—why would you have shoved me like that?" *Shut up! Stop talking! You're making a fool of yourself!* "I mean, I haven't done anything to you," my voice continued, ignoring the instructions from my brain. "Why would you do that?"

"Like *I've* never been shoved," Daisy muttered. Her face was scrunched up, her cheeks red and angry. "Or thrown out of a *window!*"

"What?"

"Nothing."

She stormed off again. I practically had to run to keep up with her. "What did you say? Something about being thrown out of a window?" Someone must have done something terrible to Daisy. It was no wonder she was so angry.

"Forget it," she said.

"But that's awful!" I said gently. "I mean, it's really terrible, Daisy. Who would do something like that to you? Who *could* do something so awful?"

Daisy stopped walking for a second and looked into my eyes. "I *wonder!*" she said pointedly before marching off again—her limp even more pronounced as she stomped away.

I caught up with her and put a hand on her arm. We both stopped where we were. "Daisy, tell me, why did you shove me?" I asked.

Daisy shook me off. "It's my job, OK?" she snapped. "That's what I'm here for!"

Her job? "What do you mean?" I asked. I didn't want to make her even angrier, but she was talking in riddles. "I don't understand. How can it be your job to push me?"

She rolled her eyes again. "It's not my job to push you!" she said.

"But you just said it was."

"It's my job to look after you!"

"But—but it's me who's meant to be looking after you!"

"Yeah, sure it is," she sneered. Then she burst out, "Since when were you a fairy godmother?"

We stared at each other in silence, the air between us frozen and hard. I opened my mouth to reply. My jaw stayed open, but nothing came out.

"A what?" I said eventually.

"Nothing. I didn't say anything."

"Yes, you did," I insisted.

"No. I *didn't*," she repeated. "I'll get into even more trouble now. You're not supposed to tell.

They'll probably put me on traffic duty or something to punish me. Day after day sitting on airplanes next to terrified people crying their way to places all over the world. Whoop-de-do!"

What was she talking about? "Daisy, you're not making any sense," I said.

"You think you know it all, you humans," she exploded. "You don't care about anything except yourselves. Even when we're here to help you, you're ungrateful. Look what they did to FGBumblebee1167. Five minutes into his life cycle, and he was swatted dead by the client. Dead! It's not a game, you know. It's our lives at stake. He hadn't even started his assignment. And you're just as bad!"

I stared at Daisy, wondering if she needed help.

"Yes, you heard right," she snapped. "I'm your fairy godmother. And before you say anything, it wasn't my choice. It's just a job, and don't worry, I plan to get it done and be out of your life as soon as I possibly can."

"My what?" I said with a gasp. "But—but . . ." My words dried up into a big fat silence that sat awkwardly in between us. "You can't be my fairy godmother," I said eventually.

"Oh, really? Why's that?"

"Well, I mean, apart from anything else, you're the same age as me." I put aside the whole issue of the existence of fairies — it didn't seem like a great idea to push it at this stage.

"Really? What makes you think that?"

"Well, you *look* my age."

Daisy folded her arms. "We materialize at whatever age is appropriate for our assignments. And for this one, I'm a girl like you," she said. "Well, not *exactly* like you, obviously," she added, looking me up and down as if I were a piece of dirt. "But close enough."

I looked back at her. I didn't care if she'd just "materialized" as a girl. She looked my age — not my mother's! "I'm still not going to call you my fairy godmother," I said. "It doesn't sound right."

Daisy sighed. "OK, forget the whole 'mother' thing if it bothers you that much," she said. "Think of me as your fairy godsister."

"But there's no such thing!"

"Oh, really? What am I, then? A figment of your imagination?"

Just then, the afternoon bell rang loudly down the hallway. "It doesn't make me any happier than it makes you," she said quickly. "But we're stuck together for now, so we might as well get to work."

"Get to work on what?"

"The assignment. The quicker the assignment's done, the sooner I'm out of here," she went on. "Then we can both put the whole thing behind us and never have to see each other again."

I swallowed. "OK," I said. I still didn't know what she was talking about, but if she wanted it over and done with — whatever "it" was — well, then, so did I!

"Good," Daisy replied.

"Fine," I said.

"Fine!" she replied more sharply. Then we headed back to the classroom without exchanging another word.

I spent the afternoon in a fog of confusion. Daisy and I didn't speak to each other again all day. We hardly even looked at each other. A couple of times, Miss Holdsworth asked me a question and I had no idea what to say. I didn't even know what she'd asked me. I couldn't concentrate on anything except what Daisy had told me.

I kept sneaking sideways glances at her, hoping I

could get my brain to understand what was happening. She was my fairy godmother? Was it possible? *Could* it be true? I mean, a couple of days ago, I was totally prepared to believe that fairies existed — but then I'd come to my senses! Girls my age don't believe in fairy godmothers! Or fairy godsisters, or whatever she was. It just wasn't possible.

But then there was that incident in the hallway. I could have had a really bad accident if she hadn't shoved me just then.

Coincidence. It *must* have been.

It was just some fancy trick. I wouldn't be surprised if Trisha Miles was behind it somehow. Just a new way to make fun of me.

For the millionth time that day, I wished that Charlotte was there. I could have told her about it, and she'd have laughed at me again and told me all the reasons why fairy godmothers don't logically, scientifically exist — never mind fairy godsisters. I laughed at myself, just imagining Charlotte's voice gently chiding me.

But there was a tiny nagging thought at the back of my mind. It was just out of reach, and I was happy for it to stay that way. I didn't want to be troubled by doubt, so I ignored it, and by the end of the afternoon I'd pretty much put the whole conversation out of my mind. Whatever the new girl was up to, I wasn't going to let her make a fool out of me.

I had my parents to do that.

I could see the bright yellow van the second I stepped out of school. I slunk across the playground, praying, as I always prayed, that they wouldn't sound the horn.

Trisha's mom was at the gates in her new BMW convertible. I looked around for Daisy, wondering who would be picking her up and where she lived. Then I caught myself. What was I doing thinking about her? She wasn't important. She was just someone else who wanted to make me look stupid.

I climbed into the van. Mom smiled brightly at me. "Good day, hon?" she asked, like she always does.

"It was OK," I said as I closed the door behind me.

"Philippa!"

Someone was calling me from outside the van. I looked down. Daisy! What did she want now? To make me look like an idiot again? I rolled down the window. "What?" I asked curtly.

She was holding a large envelope out. "Take this," she said, thrusting the envelope through the window. It was a shiny metallic color, with swirling pinks and blues and purples. The colors all seemed to glow and move as you looked at them, like a hologram.

"What is it?" I asked.

"Just take it. I'll explain later. You need to have it, though."

Mom leaned across me. "Hello, there," she said. "Are you a new friend of Philippa's? I haven't met you before."

"I'm Daisy," Daisy said. "I just started school here today."

I grabbed the envelope. "OK, see you tomorrow," I said, rolling the window up before Mom could say anything to embarrass me and make matters even worse.

Mom smiled at Daisy. "Bye, Daisy," she called. "See you again, I hope."

Not if I could help it!

As we drove away, I looked down at the envelope. My hand tingled and burned where I was holding it, as if there were an electric current running through my fingers. The tingling spread up my arm and ran all the way through my body. It felt so strange. Not only that, it felt familiar. When had I felt it before?

Then I remembered. *When I'd picked the daisy.*

I spun around in my seat to look back at the playground. Daisy was still there. She'd gotten her cell phone out again and was sending someone a text or playing a game on it.

What was going on? Who was she? *What* was she?

I couldn't concentrate on anything as we drove home. I put the envelope in my backpack and tried to forget about it. I hadn't decided what to do with it. I didn't even know if I was going to open it. The thought of it made me shiver.

I let Mom spend the journey telling me about her day at the shop. In some ways, Mom's the more normal of my parents. I mean, she's just as wacky as Dad in her own way; she's just not quite as loud about it. She wears horrendous clothes that make me cringe if I'm out in public with her — purple baggy tie-dyed pants and scruffy T-shirts with political slogans on them. And then there's the weird food, and the dancing, and everything. She's just not like normal moms. I mean, I love her. And

I'd never want to hurt her feelings. But I wish my parents would think about my feelings sometimes and try to blend in a bit more.

I guess she and Dad are a good match, and they get along well—which I should be grateful for. I don't think I've ever heard them argue in my whole life. At least our home is a happy place. But I can't help sometimes wishing that they didn't have to be so . . . well, so bonkers.

Mom doesn't usually honk the horn when she's picking me up, but she has been known to turn up in one of the shop's costumes when she comes straight from work. I mean, how many kids have to worry about their mother turning up at school dressed as a witch?

For now, I wasn't worried about Mom. My mind was occupied elsewhere. What was I going to do with the envelope? And how did the envelope, the tingling, the new girl, and the flower I'd picked fit together?

I went straight to my room when we got home. My daisy chain had wilted even more. It made me think of Charlotte and hope she still had hers. At least the flower in the eggcup was looking fine.

I wished I could call or e-mail her. But her parents had given up "newfangled" things like phones and computers with the move. I wanted to talk to her so badly. Did she miss me? What had she been doing since she left?

I slumped down on my bed, desperately hoping I'd hear from her soon. Opening my bag, I took the envelope out. It sparkled and shone, sending tiny rainbows all around my room as it caught the sunlight through the window.

I sat staring at it for ages. I kept making up my mind to open it, but as soon as I picked it up, I changed my mind again. What if there was something really bad inside? What if I opened it and released an evil spirit and I'd never be free of it?

Charlotte would know what to do. *Why* did she have to leave?

I left the envelope on the bed and tried to think about something else. I emptied out my backpack. We didn't have any homework. We never got any on the first day back after vacation. For once I wished that we did, so I could have something to occupy my mind.

It wouldn't have worked, anyway. No matter

what else I did, I could feel the envelope burning through it all, asking to be opened. There was a link with the flower; I knew it. There were too many coincidences for there not to be. Like Daisy's name, for a start! And the tingling feeling I got from the envelope feeling just like the tingling I got from the daisy.

And the bruises on Daisy's arm. She said she'd been thrown out of a window.

A tree-house window?

I sat down on my bed and breathed hard. The realization took my breath away.

It was true. There was no getting around it. Daisy really was a fairy.

I opened the envelope. As I did, colors flew out from inside it, popping and crackling like fireworks. A streak of yellow shot across my bedroom like a lightning bolt. Pink waves spun out in a circle, whizzing around and around in front of my face. Blue spots jumped and danced like electric raindrops plinking onto the floor.

I shut the envelope again quickly. Mom was bound to hear. I couldn't open it in the house.

The tree house. I'd open it there.

I shoved the envelope under my sweater and sneaked through the kitchen. Mom was on the phone in the front room. I didn't want to have to explain anything. I just wanted to be by myself.

Clutching the envelope tightly, I stepped onto the ladder at the bottom of the tree house. Something caught my eye above me, and I looked up. Light. It looked as if there were a firework display going on inside the tree house! Cracking and snapping and whizzing sounds spun around above my head. Light shot out in sparks, dancing to the popping noise.

My first thought was to scream, "FIRE!" and run to the house to get Mom.

My second thought was: *This is what Dad saw.* Whatever was going on in there, I realized it was connected with what Dad had seen on Saturday night.

My legs trembled as I inched upward, creeping up the rungs as quietly as I could. My heart banged so hard that it felt as if someone were hitting my chest.

A couple more steps and then I leaned forward,

craning my neck to look inside. And then I looked up — and saw her.

Daisy! She was inside my tree house! What was she doing?

I crouched low, out of sight, and craned my neck to watch. She'd taken her sweater off at last. She was wearing a beautiful white top. It looked as if it were made of feathers! She looked strange without her sweater on. Her shoulder blades stuck out, like two lumps on her back. A white shimmering light flickered all around her body. What was that?

Daisy stretched and seemed to be talking to herself. I couldn't hear what she was saying, but as she spoke, the most incredible thing happened: The light seemed to grow into her clothes, into her body. And then something even stranger happened. Something was growing out of her jutting shoulder blades.

Wings! As delicate as the finest silk you could imagine. Patterned in swirling rainbow colors, the edges were soft feathers in pink and purple and turquoise.

I stared and stared, for a moment forgetting

everything else in the world. All I could think was, *It's true. Daisy is my fairy!*

And then she turned around.

"YOU!" she exclaimed, spotting me. "What are *you* doing here?"

She backed away to the opposite edge of the tree house, folding her arms defiantly and pursing her lips in an angry frown. The scowl didn't suit her in the same way that it had at school. It's not easy to look hard and tough when you're wearing a shimmering, sparkling feathery top and you have the most beautiful wings in the world sticking out of your back.

"You're a fairy," I said simply, smiling at her despite everything. "You're my fairy."

"I am not *your* fairy!" she burst out. "Don't *ever* say that again!"

"I — but I thought you —"

"Yes, I know what you *thought*," Daisy snapped. "You thought you could just pick me and own me, and that I'd follow along behind you, doing everything you want. You thought what fun it would be to have a fairy all your own, and how you'd have me at your beck and call, and how special I'd make your life. Didn't you?"

I didn't know what to say. She was right. I had thought she would be my fairy, and I did think it would make my life special. Was that so wrong?

"Thought so," she said. "Well, I've got news for you, so you'd better listen."

"I am listening," I said in a whisper. My throat hurt. Why was she being so mean?

"It's my job. OK? It's just a job. I'll be here for as long as it takes to get my assignment done — and I plan on getting it done in record time, since I'd rather not hang around here too long. Do you get it?"

I nodded. I didn't get it at all, though. What did she mean — it was a job? What was the assignment? I didn't dare ask. I didn't want her to bite my head off any more than she already was doing.

"And I'll be living in here for the duration of the assignment. Any problems with that?"

I shook my head. I felt happier about that — she might not be my very own fairy, but she was living in my tree house. She'd be right here for as long as it took for her to do her assignment, whatever that meant. There really would be a fairy living in my backyard!

"No problem," I said, suppressing a smile.

"Good. I'm glad that's all clear," she said.

"Can I come up, then?" I asked.

Daisy shrugged. "You might as well."

I climbed up the remaining rungs and pulled myself through the trapdoor. As I did so, Daisy pointed to the envelope sticking out from under my sweater.

"You haven't opened it yet?" she asked.

I shook my head. "That's why I came to the tree house. I wanted to do it here." I pulled the envelope out and put it down on the tree-house floor between us.

"OK, go ahead," Daisy said. I know I could have imagined it, but I'm sure she sounded nervous. Her voice wobbled slightly as she added, "Open the envelope, and let's get this assignment started."

chapter five

WISH VOUCHERS

Colors leaped from the envelope as soon as I opened it, exactly as they'd done in my bedroom. Pink, purple, turquoise, yellow—every color you could imagine swirled like a living rainbow around the tree house.

I reached inside the envelope and pulled the contents out. Three shiny pieces of paper. At least, they looked like paper, but they felt more like satin. Smooth and shiny, they were as colorful as the lights dancing all around us, shimmering and glittering in my hands. There was something written across each one. When I looked closer, I could see a line of strange symbols.

"What are they?" I asked.

"Turn them over."

I did what she said and looked at the first one. Right in the center of the dancing colors were two words in swirly pink lettering:

I looked up at Daisy. "I don't understand," I said.

"What is there not to understand?" she asked in the same irritated tone that she seemed to use to say everything.

"What are they for?"

Daisy rolled her eyes. "Isn't it obvious? Honestly, you'd think 3WD would be the most straight-forward department in the air! Not with you, it isn't!"

"What's 3WD?" I asked.

"The Three Wishes Department, of course!" Daisy said, her voice rising in volume and pitch with every word. "That's what I'm here for. You've got three wishes, OK?"

I stared at Daisy, then looked back down at the vouchers in my hands. *Really? I have three wishes?* "Are you joking?" I asked in a near-whisper.

Daisy inhaled heavily through her nose. "No. I am NOT joking," she said very deliberately. "Although you are starting to really annoy me!" she added under her breath.

"But why? Why me? Why now?"

"We have categories of need. You qualified for 3WD because you were so sad."

"Because of Charlotte going away?"

Daisy nodded. "Almost everyone has a fairy godmother at some point in their lives."

"Really?"

"Of course. Not that they thank us for it. Ungrateful things, you humans."

"But—but I've never heard anyone say they had a fairy godmother before!"

"Of course you haven't! People don't usually know about it. Fairy Godmother Code states that you should never reveal yourself to a client. You can get into serious trouble if you do."

"But you revealed yourself to me!"

"I know. I shouldn't have; it was very unprofessional of me. I'll probably get hauled over the clouds for it. You made me so angry, though. I mean, what were you *thinking*, throwing me out the window like that?"

"I'm sorry," I said, lowering my head with shame and regret. "I never would have done it if I'd known you would—"

Daisy brushed the rest of my sentence away with her hand. "Forget it," she said. "It's done now. But for future reference, it's not a good way to get a fairy godmother on your side."

I glanced up to see what looked like the tiniest hint of a smile at the edge of Daisy's mouth. Was she joking? Maybe she'd forgiven me!

My face broke into a wide grin—until she added, "So don't be getting any ideas that we're going to be buddies, because we're not. Remember, you're just a job to me. Nothing more. Nothing less. An assignment. OK?"

My face fell back into the miserable expression it had worn for most of the last couple of days. "OK," I said limply. "But just tell me this — is it really true that everyone has a fairy godmother?"

"Pretty much," Daisy replied. "Some people have one just for a short job like this one. Others have one by their side for years. It depends on how long her life cycle is."

"Life cycle? What's that?"

"You materialize as something from nature for each assignment. And whatever you come from in nature determines how long you have to do your work."

"So you mean you have as long as a daisy's normal life span? That's the whole summer, isn't it?"

"Well, not exactly."

"Why not?"

"Because I've been picked. It's the life span of a picked daisy."

"A picked daisy? But that's hardly anything!"

"I should get a week and a half if I'm careful — that's plenty of time for 3WD."

"And what happens if you don't get your assignment done in time?"

"That's not a question you want to ask. It's certainly not something I'd want to put to the test."

"Why?"

"Well, what happens at the end of someone's life cycle?"

I thought about it. "They die?" I said, hoping I wasn't stating the obvious.

"Exactly," Daisy said sharply.

"You'll *die*?" Surely I'd heard that wrong.

Daisy shrugged, but her face had turned a little paler, her mouth a little tighter.

"Comes with the territory," she said matter-of-factly. "Now, can we move on?" And with that, the subject was clearly closed.

I wanted to ask more. The stakes were so high! It felt like too much responsibility. I'd have to make sure that I made my wishes as quickly as I could.

"So you were saying," I prompted her, to change the subject in the hope that she would stop being so snappy. "Everyone has a fairy godmother?"

"Pretty much."

"Even my mom and dad might have had one?"

Daisy picked up her bag and took out her cell

phone. "Hang on," she said, pressing a few buttons. As I watched over her shoulder, I could see that it wasn't a cell phone at all. It had about twice as many buttons as a phone, and the screen flashed and sparkled just like the vouchers had.

"What's that?" I asked.

Daisy looked up. "This? It's my MagiCell."

"What's a magisell?"

"MagiCell." Daisy spelled it out for me. "It's a fairy godmother's most essential piece of equipment. It gives me all the information I need for my assignment. Any background information or reference points — I can get them all on this. And about a trazillion other things besides. I'm just looking up your parents."

Daisy pressed a few buttons. "Ah, got your mom. No, she hasn't had one yet. Well, not really. Seems she had a sighting a long time ago."

"A sighting? What's that?"

"She stumbled upon some fairies practicing a new spell and overheard part of it."

I thought of the song Mom had sung with me when I was little. Was that it? Surely not!

"Luckily, she only learned one verse, not the whole thing," Daisy continued. "But it looks like the song might have helped fast-track you through the FGD." Daisy looked up. "Fairy Godmother Department, that is," she added. "That would have helped you get such a good department to help you with your sadness. Some people have to be thoroughly depressed for *years* before they get 3WD."

It was true, then! The song. Of course — it all made sense. We'd sung it so many times — and I'd been singing it to myself right before I'd picked Daisy. I'd been singing a real, actual fairy song!

Daisy was pressing more buttons on her MagiCell. "Hang on — I'll check your dad."

I watched in silence while she frowned and pressed more buttons. "Yeah, your dad had one, way back. Fifteen years ago, it says here. Oh, he had someone from 1GTD."

"1GTD?" I asked. "What does that mean?" It sounded like a license plate number.

"One Good Turn Department," Daisy said. "It's where a fairy godmother does you a good turn in exchange for one that you've done for them. I haven't got much information here. It just has key words: *apple, beggar, hut.*" Daisy looked up. "Mean anything to you?"

I thought for a second. *Apple, beggar, hut* — what did that mean? Then I realized. The beggar! But hang on — that was an old man!

"Can fairy godmothers be male?" I asked, feeling foolish.

"Of course. *Fairy godmother* is a generic term. And anyway, like I said before, we materialize in whatever form is appropriate for the task."

"Wow!" I said. "That's how my dad met my mom. And he doesn't even know?"

"Nope. They never do. Well, usually. OK, look — to be perfectly honest with you, I've never *actually* worked with humans before. 3WD is a hard assignment, since you have to find a way to give your clients their vouchers without them knowing. I'm sure I'll get better at it — if they let me do it again."

Daisy's voice had softened. It felt as if she were opening up a bit, and I didn't want to say anything that might ruin the moment and chase her away again. I sat looking down at the vouchers. "How do they work?" I asked finally.

"Self-explanatory," she said. "Each voucher gives you a wish. Three vouchers, three wishes."

"As simple as that?"

"Nearly. You have to make them at the right time, or the results can be unpredictable." She pressed a few more buttons on her MagiCell. "Do you have something you can put the vouchers in?" she asked without looking up.

I rummaged around on the floor and picked up a wooden box with swirling orange and yellow patterns on it. "Will this do?"

Daisy glanced up. "Perfect."

I emptied out the contents. The box was full of plays that Charlotte and I had started writing together and notes we'd left each other. I felt a pang in my chest. Would I hear from her soon?

"Got it," Daisy said, pulling my attention back to the wish vouchers. "First chance is tomorrow night — 11:11 P.M. precisely."

"What happens then?"

"It's the next shooting star. It'll come from the east," she said, pointing to the window that looked out toward the woods. "Over there. You have to make your wish at the time of the shooting star."

"What's so special about a shooting star?"

Daisy spluttered as if she were about to choke. She reached over to her bag and pulled out a bottle of water. Pulling the lid off, she took a few large gulps. "What's so special about a shooting star?" she said, wiping her mouth. Her voice had regained the sharp edge it had been starting to lose. "It's only the moment when all the wishes in the world are being gathered and taken back to ATC!"

"What's ATC?"

"Above the Clouds. It's the top level of fairy-godmother control. All sorts of things take place there. As far as you're concerned, it's where the wishes are turned into reality. That's where your wishes will go when you make them."

"How will I know if I've done it at the right time?" I asked.

"Don't worry; you'll know. You can't miss it. You'd better keep the vouchers here. I don't think it would be a good idea to do it in the house. They can be noisy. And very colorful! If you watch carefully, you might even see your wish join the others as they whiz across the sky. It's quite something to see."

"Wow," I said. It was probably not the most intelligent or exciting thing I could have said at that point, but to be honest with you, there just weren't any other words in my mind. I looked down at the wishes, then I looked up at Daisy. The colors, the sparkling, it was all still going on around us and had been doing so throughout the whole conversation, gently flowing and floating on the air while we talked.

I tried to think of something smart to say. "Wow," I said again.

I lay in bed, nowhere near asleep. Mom and Dad had gone to bed ages ago. The house was silent, sleeping, too. It felt as though the whole world were asleep except me.

What was I going to wish for? I had a day to decide. My head was spinning with possibilities. Then I remembered something Mom had once told me. When she can't sleep, she says, she gets out a piece of paper and writes down everything on her mind. Once it's on paper, it stops racing around in her head, and she usually goes back to sleep. It was worth a try.

I flicked on the light and crept out of bed. Pulling my planner out of my book bag, I grabbed a pen and climbed back into bed. Then I made a list.

THINGS I COULD WISH FOR

1. World peace

Too corny. I mean, don't get me wrong. World peace would be good. Well, it would be really, *really* good — amazing in fact. But to be honest, I wasn't convinced that world peace could suddenly come about from a wish of mine, and I didn't want to waste any of my vouchers.

2. Winning the lottery

OK, there were a couple of problems with this one. The first was that I was too young to play the lottery, so I'd obviously never bought a ticket. The second was that Mom and Dad didn't believe in it, so they'd never bought a ticket, either. So that one was kind of out as well.

3. Winning a million dollars by some other means

This one had potential. I chewed the end of my

pen and considered it for a moment. What would I do if I had a million dollars?

Well, first I'd give half of it to Mom and Dad so they could pay off the mortgage and maybe even get a new van that wasn't quite so embarrassing, and Mom could give up working at the shop, so I'd never need to worry about her turning up at school in costume again. Then I'd buy lots of games and books, and I'd buy the best tricks you could get, so I could do amazing magic.

Except for one problem. Charlotte was the only person I ever did my tricks in front of, and she wasn't around. So, I decided against the million dollars idea.

I sat looking at the page for a while, thinking about the next possibility. I knew what I wanted to write. I just wanted it too much even to write it down.

4. Charlotte moving back

There—I'd written it. It was what I wanted more than anything. But I knew I couldn't really wish for it. It wasn't fair. Charlotte had been so excited about her family's new life. I knew she missed me; I didn't doubt that. But she wanted to live on a farm, and she had always adored ponies more than anything in the world, and she desperately wanted a puppy, too, and now she was going to have all of it.

I couldn't take it away from her, never mind destroy her parents' dream. No. I wasn't wishing for that. I tore a page out of my planner. It was time I tried to get in touch with her.

> *Dear Charlotte,*
> *I miss you sooooooooooooooooooo much.*

I paused. What could I say next? *I've discovered that I've got a fairy godmother and she's granted me three wishes?* Charlotte would die laughing. And for once, I didn't want to make her laugh. This was serious.

I put my pen down and closed my eyes for a moment. Before I knew it, my planner had fallen on the floor, the wishes had turned to wings, my bedroom had become a cloud, and I was flying. . . .

I drifted off into a deep sleep.

chapter six
DECISION

Someone was shouting from down on the ground. I turned over on my cloud, pulling its fluffy corners over my face.

They kept calling. The cloud drifted away. I was falling down, falling fast — *thump!*

I landed on my bed.

I opened my eyes, rubbing them as I looked around at my surroundings. I wasn't on a cloud at all. Just in my ordinary bedroom.

Mom was calling me. Her voice drifted into my consciousness, and I forced my eyes open. Why was she calling me in the middle of the night? And how come it was light outside?

I glanced at my bedside clock. It was nearly eight thirty. I'd overslept.

"Philippa, are you up, honey?" Mom's voice was coming from outside my bedroom.

Her face poked around the door. Her hair was tousled and her cheeks red and creased. "Darling, you're going to be late for school," she said, her voice groggy and heavy. "I'm so sorry; we slept in."

Of *course* they slept in. They always do if I don't wake them!

"I didn't hear my alarm," I replied sleepily. "I'll be down in a second."

"I'll get you some muesli," Mom replied. "Hurry up, now."

That was a treat! Mom fixing my breakfast, that is, not the muesli itself. If you'd ever tasted our muesli, you'd know it could never be described as a treat.

Dad drove to school like a maniac, breaking the speed limit and running a couple of red lights.

"Dad, it's OK if I'm a few minutes late," I said gently, hoping he'd understand that actually I meant I wanted him to slow down and be more careful so that I could at least show up at school alive.

"Don't you worry about that," he said, turning to me as he spoke. I really wish he wouldn't do that. Dad can't drive without talking to you all the time. And he can't talk without looking at you. Which makes being in a car with him fairly dangerous, if you think about it. I try not to.

Watch the road! I urged silently.

"I'll get you there on time," he added. "Don't want you arriving after everyone else and standing out, do we?"

I stifled a laugh. Dad was trying to make sure I didn't stand out? What kind of a planet did he live on where bright yellow vans and hyperactive dads and hippie tie-dyed moms didn't make a girl stand out?

I'd never say anything, though. I could just imagine his face crumpling if I did, and I didn't want to upset him — or Mom. It was OK; the van wasn't that bad. If you closed your eyes. And your ears.

We arrived at school just after the bell rang. I'd missed attendance. I jumped out of the van and was about to close the door and say good-bye when Dad shut the engine off.

"What are you doing?" I asked.

"I don't want you getting into trouble. I'll come

in and talk to your teacher. I'll tell her it was my fault."

"But it *wasn't* your fault!" I screeched, horrified. He wasn't really going to come in and talk to my teacher in front of the whole class, was he?

"It was, sweetheart. Your mother and I are responsible for you. We shouldn't have slept in. It's up to us to make sure you get to school on time. We're your parents!"

"But Dad—"

He shook his head. "No buts; I'm coming in." And with that, he closed his door, locked the van, and walked over to join me. It was only then that I realized something completely awful.

Dad was wearing his pajamas.

"Dad! You can't come into school like that!"

"It's fine," he said, waving a hand casually to bat my horror away. "No one will know they're pajamas. Hey, I think they look trendy, like the kind of baggy pants the kids all wear today. Don't you?"

There were so many reasons why what Dad had said was wrong. I couldn't even begin to go into them, so instead I said nothing. I just hoped I'd be able to think of something before we actually got into school. He couldn't, in all honesty, be proposing that he walk into my classroom with me, in front of everyone, and talk to my teacher in his pajamas, could he? I mean, he couldn't. Even my dad wouldn't go that far.

"So, like I said, it wasn't Philippa's fault at all, and it won't happen again."

Dad smiled widely at Miss Holdsworth, totally oblivious to the fact that the entire class was staring at him. Some were just looking at him in shock. Others were whispering. I heard one boy say, "Tell me that guy isn't in his pajamas." I didn't hear the reply. I didn't want to. What I actually wanted more than anything in the world at that precise moment was to crawl under my table and transport myself to a different world. A world where I didn't have any parents. Or if I did, they were *normal*.

There was something else, too. Seeing everyone's eyes on Dad like that, all of them snickering behind their hands, brought something up. A memory. The worst memory.

No! I wasn't going to think about that. I'd never think about that again.

I dragged my mind back to the present — which was only marginally better. Dad turned and winked at me as he left. "See you tonight, pumpkin," he said.

I couldn't reply. My face was about to blow up from the heat it was generating. Had he really, truly, honestly just done that? Had my dad *really* just come into my class in front of everyone, in his pajamas, talked to my teacher, and called me *pumpkin* on the way out?

I turned to Daisy on the off chance that I might receive some kind of a sympathetic look. She looked at me with no emotion on her face at all. She must have been the only person in the class not laughing or looking mortified. Maybe Dad's kind of behavior was normal where she came from. Maybe it was standard practice in the fairy world for people to walk around in their pajamas.

I glanced at Lauren and Beth. Surely they'd give me a bit of support. But both of them were looking down, arranging and rearranging the books and pencils on their desks. They both looked almost as embarrassed as I did.

Miss Holdsworth clapped her hands. "All right, then, 6B, let's get down to some work, shall we? Open your French books to chapter seven."

We'd only started French this year. Part of getting

us ready for high school, they said. I didn't normally like it, but today I was grateful for anything that would take my mind off what had just happened.

Everyone rummaged around in their bags and desks, getting out their books, until Miss Holdsworth clapped her hands again. "Settle down, 6B," she said sternly. Normally, that was enough to get everyone listening. No one wanted to be on the receiving end of one of her tirades. But the stern voice wasn't working today. A snorting, giggling, muffled sound was inching around the room. I looked to my side without lifting my head. I still couldn't bear to show my face to the class. Everyone at the next table had their hands over their mouths, stifling giggles.

It was only when I opened my book that I realized why:

"Chapter Seven: The Family."

There was a picture of a mother and father with their son and daughter. And the father was wearing a pair of striped pants almost exactly like the ones my dad had been wearing.

Tyrone Goulden put his hand up. "Miss, what's French for blue-striped pajamas?" he asked, at which the entire class burst out laughing. The entire class except for my table, that is. Lauren and Beth looked embarrassed, Daisy responded with the same haughty expression she had for most things, and I just wanted to die on the spot.

Even Miss Holdsworth had to suppress a smile. "Come on, now, 6B," she said. "Let's get down to some sensible work."

I spent the rest of the morning trying to figure out ways that I could avoid having to show my face at school ever again. I drifted off into my own little world, which is what I usually do when something's making me unhappy.

I created some imaginary parents for myself in my imaginary world. My dad was an accountant who went to work in a suit and tie. He drove a normal car, maybe a Ford Mustang or something like that. He didn't have a special horn added to the car. He had normal conversations with people about things like the weather or the state of the economy. Other than that, he kept to himself and didn't attract attention. He played squash with his boss. He got up on time. In fact, he did everything on time. He never, ever embarrassed his daughter.

My imaginary mom had a totally normal kind of job, too. She could be the personal assistant to the manager of a local law firm. She didn't make tofu rolls, and she didn't think that toasted sunflower seeds were a treat. She made all my favorite meals! She gave me chips and ham sandwiches for my lunch box, and we always had tons of chocolate cookies in a tin in the kitchen. She wore stylish clothes with designer labels, not hippie tie-dyed pants and baggy T-shirts with political slogans on them. She was tidy and cared about my education more than playing the fiddle or mending policeman outfits, and she didn't sit around in her nightgown for half the day.

If only.

Then I remembered. The wishes! I shook myself out of my dreamworld and looked at Daisy. She had a blank expression on her face that, for once, wasn't all that different from anyone else's expression. Miss Holdsworth was talking about matching verbs and nouns and gender, and half the class looked as lost as Daisy. As I watched her, I noticed her face looked slightly gray this morning. Was she OK? I hoped she wasn't ill. It might ruin my wishes! Then I felt really bad for having such a selfish thought.

I nudged her. "Daisy!" I whispered.

She turned to face me. "What?"

"I've got my first wish!" I said. "I know what I want to wish for!"

"Well, thank the clouds for that!" she said. "Finally we can get the assignment started. The sooner we get going, the quicker I'm out of here, and we can both get on with our lives."

"Yes, OK," I said, probably snapping a little more than I intended. Did she have to remind me how much she didn't want to be around me? It wasn't exactly what I needed to hear.

I wasn't going to let anything get to me today. Not Daisy with her bad mood and her angry response to everything I said. Not the rest of my classmates, who snickered behind their hands every time I caught anyone's eye.

"Got the time, Jack?" Trisha Miles said loudly to her friend Jacqui Anderson as they passed me.

Jacqui stuck her arm out to look at her watch. "Ten o'clock in the morning," she replied.

"Oooh, really? Better get into my pajamas, then,"

Trisha replied, and they went off down the corridor hooting and laughing and falling all over themselves. Yes, ha, ha. Very funny. How original.

Even Lauren and Beth seemed to be avoiding me. Well, I didn't care. I didn't have to worry about my parents anymore.

At least, I wouldn't have to after tonight.

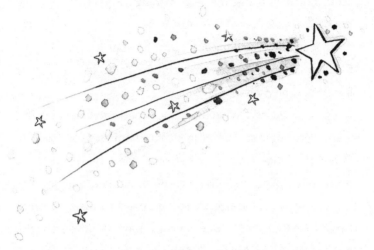

I didn't really understand what was happening at first. I mean, these clothes are all strange to me anyway. I wouldn't know someone's pajamas from his dress clothes. Who cares what humans wear? It's not my job to be bothered with things like that.

But there was something really weird going on in the class all day. I'd already gathered that Philippa's group wasn't the coolest gang around. That concerned me enough, to begin with. As it was my first human-contact task, it would have been nice to be paired up with someone in my league, like Trisha Miles or her friends. They were my kind of girls. Funny, witty, sharp, and, OK, yes, maybe a bit mean. But they didn't really do any harm. It's just a little fun, if you ask me—something to get you through the day.

It seemed that Philippa was having trouble getting through her day—without everyone in the school making fun of her, anyway.

Once I realized what had happened, my first thought was, *Well, come on.* What in cloud's name was her weirdo father thinking? I mean, what else could she expect? It's practically *asking* the whole school to make fun of you.

But this really bizarre thing happened to me as soon as I had that thought. It was almost a pain. A little stab. But not on my body. More—I don't know; I can't describe it. Almost like a little trip of a switch in my head that made me itch. A thought. A strange thought. The kind of thought I've never had before, so I didn't recognize it. Or maybe a feeling. And I'm not really used to that.

I mean, obviously I have feelings. I've been angry quite a lot. When my friend died, I was furious with the human who did it. But this felt different. It was like being sad, only it was as if I were feeling someone else's sadness, not even my own.

I guess I felt sorry for her. Not such a complicated emotion, really.

Crazy, huh? Girl throws me out of a window, gets three wishes—from *me*—and I feel sorry for her! What was happening to me? I was turning as nutty as her and her crazy parents.

So my next thought was: *Just keep your head down, get the wishes done, and get out of this place before the life cycle's up.*

I could already feel it getting to me. I felt weaker than yesterday, and I wasn't managing to get enough water. It wasn't like in training. And if I was totally honest, real live humans weren't quite as I'd imagined. At least, Philippa wasn't.

At lunchtime I spent ten minutes guzzling nonstop from the water fountain in the hall, trying to revive myself, until I realized there was a line of people waiting. At least I felt a bit stronger afterward. Which was just as well, because in the afternoon things got even worse. It wasn't just Philippa they were making fun of. They started in on our whole table. Me and those other girls, Lauren and Beth.

Hang on a minute! Don't you be making fun of ME! I wanted to shout. *I'm not like her! I'm not one of them! I'm Fairy Godmother 92751 from 3WD. A FAIRY GODMOTHER! I'm not some boring, geeky girl with crazy parents who does magic tricks on her own and who can't even get her best friend to stay in the same town!*

And then it happened again, as soon as I'd thought all

that. The weird feeling. I could see Philippa out of the corner of my eye, pulling her brown mop of hair over her face as though she could hide behind it, afraid to come out.

It wasn't her fault. I shouldn't think mean thoughts about her.

For the second time in about half an hour, I shook myself. What was I *doing*, feeling sorry for her? I really had to get a grip before I became as soft as Philippa. And I really had to get out of here soon.

I picked up my reading book and propped it up on my desk so the teacher couldn't see what I was doing. Then I got out my MagiCell and pushed a few buttons to double-check my life-cycle prediction.

EIGHT DAYS, it flashed. That took me to next Wednesday. Just a week and a half, and then I'd be out of here. Good.

Next Wednesday couldn't come soon enough.

chapter seven
SHOOTING STAR

I ran out of school the second Miss Holdsworth said we could go. I didn't say good-bye to anyone, not even Lauren or Beth. Or Daisy. Not that she'd care. She hardly talked to me all afternoon.

I raced across the playground before anyone else came out. I couldn't go through it all again. As soon as they saw the van, they'd say something; I knew it.

I prayed that at least it would be Mom who would pick me up. Just one more time, that was all I had to get through. It would be different tomorrow.

The van was there, just outside the gates — and thank goodness, it was Mom.

"Good day, hon?" she asked as usual. I couldn't answer. I couldn't even speak. How could I begin to explain what kind of a day I'd had?

Eventually, I muttered, "Mmm," and thankfully that was good enough for her. She started talking about a man who'd come into the shop looking for an outfit to wear when he proposed to his girlfriend. Apparently the girlfriend was a big Superman fan, and he'd decided he was going to dress up as Superman to pop the question. They didn't have any adult-size costumes, so he had to think again. I didn't really hear what he decided in the end. I'd tuned out by then. I was too busy planning my first wish.

Nine thirty. Nearly two hours to go. What if I fell asleep? Daisy didn't tell me when the next shooting star was after tonight. I couldn't afford to miss this one. I simply *couldn't* go through another day like today. The thought of it jolted me into alertness. I wouldn't fall asleep. No way!

I decided to practice one of the tricks from *The Magician's Handbook* while I waited for the next couple of hours to pass: "How to Magnetize Your Hand." I picked up a pencil from the floor and held it out in one hand, wrapping the other hand around my wrist like it said in the book. I stuck out my finger, sneakily holding the pencil in place against my palm. From the other side, it looked like the pencil was sticking magically to my palm. Cool!

It wasn't the same without Charlotte to watch, though. She was always so impressed whenever I had a new trick. I guess I understand why Dad enjoys doing what he does: It's so great seeing people's faces full of amazement when you impress them. Not that I'd ever perform in front of anyone ever again.

I put the pencil away. As I did, I noticed the daisy in my eggcup. The water had gone down a bit, so I added some more. "Come on, little daisy," I said to the drooping flower. "I want you to stay alive."

Now that I knew all about Daisy's assignment, the flower didn't just represent my friendship with Charlotte. It was also a reminder of Daisy's life cycle. She would probably live as long as this flower did. She needed to look after herself to last as long as possible, and I would look after this little daisy, too. It would be a constant reminder of the urgency of Daisy's task.

Ten fifteen. Only an hour to go. I picked up *The Magician's Handbook* from the floor by my bed and was soon engrossed in the next trick: "How to Make a Calculator Predict the Future."

It seemed like it was only five minutes later when I next looked at my clock, but it read five minutes to eleven. Nearly time!

I put my book away and pulled on my bathrobe. I had to sneak down to the tree house without disturbing Mom and Dad. And I had to get there in the next ten minutes!

I softly opened my bedroom door and crept out onto the landing. The house was silent. Mom and Dad were in their bedroom, but I could see the light on under their door. I tiptoed past and slunk down the stairs, holding my breath. I hoped they wouldn't hear my heart hammering in the silent house.

Five past eleven. Quick! I snuck across the kitchen and unlocked the back door. Once I'd shut it carefully behind me, I bolted through the yard and clambered up the ladder.

"Daisy?"

"I'm up here," she called down.

I pulled myself up through the trapdoor.

"I thought you were going to miss it," Daisy said sharply.

I was starting to get used to her saying things sharply; she didn't seem to say them any other way.

"Here," she said, passing me the box with the wish vouchers inside before I had a chance to answer her.

I took the envelope out of the box. Misty colors flapped around my hands, dancing on my fingers like a soft breeze. I stared, still not one hundred percent sure that any of this was real.

"Come on, you've only got two minutes," she urged.

11:10. A minute to go. I held the wish voucher in my hand and looked at Daisy.

"That way," she said, pointing out the window that overlooked the woods. That one faced east, the direction the shooting star was going to come from any second now. My heart galloped in my chest; my hand trembled as I held the wish out; my watch ticked the seconds away.

11:11. *Please let this be true. Please make it work.* I thrust my arm right out the window, holding the voucher in my hand, and prayed that the shooting star wouldn't be late.

"Go," Daisy said with a nod.

This was it! "I wish that I could change my parents!" I said out loud. "Make them exactly how I imagined them this morning!"

The second I'd finished speaking, the voucher flew from my hand.

No! Had I dropped it? "What's happened?" I asked.

"It's OK. See?" Daisy said. I looked where she was pointing. I hadn't dropped the voucher at all. There it was, shining in bright, vivid colors, lighting up the night sky as it flew away from me, away from the tree house, up toward the stars. I watched till my eyes watered. It was like a magnificent firework display shooting across the sky. It was like a rocket blasting into space: colors dancing and crackling and zooming away into the night.

And then I saw the shooting star, bolting across the sky in a flash of white light. In an instant, the dancing colors were swallowed up by the star. The voucher vanished into the bright light; a moment later the night was pure blackness again.

I'd done it. I'd made my first wish.

I left Daisy punching buttons on her MagiCell and crept back into the house as silently as I could. Mom and Dad's light was off now and I could hear Dad snoring gently as I tiptoed past.

I shivered as I got back into bed, even though it was a warm night. What had I done? Would it work? Would I know right away? How long would it be before the wish took effect? And why hadn't I asked Daisy these questions?

My mind swirled and spun, and I fell into a restless sleep, waking three or four times before morning. Each time I woke, the night seemed to grow darker, the house more silent, my head more full of questions.

What was that smell?

My nostrils woke before the rest of me. Bacon. Someone was cooking bacon. Mom would be so mad! She's been vegetarian forever!

I squinted at my alarm clock. Six thirty. I was about to turn over and catch a bit more sleep when I became aware of something else. Classical music. It was coming from downstairs. No one ever listens to classical music in our house! It's always Celtic pipe bands and Chilean drummers or Irish folk music with a political message.

What was going on?

Then I remembered the voucher and the shooting star. Was this because of my wish?

I jumped out of bed and threw on my bathrobe. I pulled back the curtains just to check that the outside world hadn't changed. It hadn't. At least, most of it hadn't. Something had, though. It was there — for real. Sitting in the driveway. A black, shiny Ford Mustang!

It had worked! It had really worked!

I ran downstairs and burst into the kitchen.

There was a man who looked kind of similar to Dad sitting at the table. Similar, yet *so* different. For one thing, his hair was short and neat. And was that gel in it?

For another, he was wearing a suit and looking clean and tidy — and awake! He was just finishing off his breakfast and reading the *Financial Times*.

He smiled at me. "Morning, sweetheart," he said in Dad's voice. "Better get yourself dressed. We don't want to be late."

I stared at him. Did he remember yesterday? Was he even the same person? Did he know that if it wasn't for me, he'd probably never in his life have gotten me to school on time?

"Cat got your tongue?" Mom said from behind me. I whirled around to see a woman who I guessed had to be Mom. Again, the resemblance was there. Just barely. But she was dressed! And cooking! I've never seen Mom in anything but her nightgown before midday. And I couldn't remember the last time we'd had anything but rabbit-food muesli and thinly sliced bricks for breakfast. Of course — I'd wished that she would cook my favorite meals!

"Mom?" I said shakily.

She smiled back. Mom's smile. Except perhaps a

bit tighter. As though she was in a rush, but trying not to show it. Of course! She had to get to work! If she was the mom I'd imagined, she was a PA in a local firm. She was wearing really trendy black pants and a nice top — with an apron over it. And her hair was different as well. It was kind of neat. Short. Straightened? And blond. Mom's hair had always been a kind of out-of-control frizzy brown mess, like Dad's. Between their hair genes, I'd never really stood a chance.

"What have you done to your hair?" I asked before I could stop myself.

Mom looked puzzled. "What do you mean, dear?" she said. "It's the same as always." Then she went back to the stove. "I'll finish making your breakfast, OK?" she said, cracking an egg into the frying pan. My mouth watered. I nearly dribbled down my chin.

"I'll be down in two minutes," I said, darting out of the door to get dressed.

It worked! It worked! It worked! I screeched to myself as I pulled my clothes on, leaping up and punching the air. My mom and dad were normal! They both looked respectable and ordinary. We had a normal car in the driveway! Mom was making a real breakfast!

I laughed with excitement. I wanted to call Charlotte and tell her. I wanted to run down the road screaming with joy. I wanted to hug Daisy. I wanted to tell *everyone*! My parents were normal!

Dad was still at the table when I went back downstairs. He was drinking coffee and reading the paper. "This came for you, dear," he said, passing an envelope to me. It had Charlotte's writing on it!

I ripped the envelope open. *To my bestest, bestest friend in the whole world*, it began. I wanted to laugh with pleasure.

"Sit down, hon, I'll bring your breakfast over," Mom said with a smile. I stuffed the letter in my pocket and tore into my breakfast as soon as she put it down on the table.

"Easy there, girl," Dad said sternly. *Easy there, girl?* He made me sound like a horse! "You'll give yourself indigestion," he added before I had a chance to say anything.

"Anyone would think you'd never seen a plate of breakfast before," Mom said more gently.

I looked down at the fried egg and bacon and sausages and hash browns. "Do we, um, do we have this every morning?" I asked hesitantly.

Mom laughed. "What a silly question."

I laughed, too. Yes, ha, ha. "Sorry," I said, still wondering what the answer to the silly question was.

After a while, Dad pulled his napkin out of its brass ring. Cloth napkins! We never use those! He wiped his mouth. "Darling, that was delicious," he said, leaning over to give Mom a kiss on the cheek. Then he got up from the table and straightened his tie. "Ten minutes, Philippa, OK?"

"Ten minutes?" I repeated, looking at my watch. I'd be early. I'd never been early for school!

"You know your father doesn't like to be late," Mom said after he'd gone out of the room.

"Dad!" I burst out. "Dad doesn't like to be late?"

Mom gave me a funny look. "Are you all right, Philippa?" she asked.

"What do you mean?"

She shook her head. "I don't know. You just seem a little different this morning."

I seemed different! I started to laugh. I stopped myself by stuffing my napkin in my mouth. *I* seemed different! What a joke! But then, it wasn't a joke to her at all. It was real life. Real, normal, ordinary, everyday life.

"Ready, hon?" Dad called from the hall. From the window, I watched him get into the Mustang. A moment later, I heard the engine gently humming in the driveway. Gently humming! Not clattering and banging and blasting out the tune to the Hokey Pokey. This was real, normal, everyday life for my dad, too.

Mom was still looking at me quizzically. I smiled at her, then reached out to give her a hug. "I'm absolutely fine, Mom," I said. And for once, I actually meant it.

I smiled to myself as I closed the car door behind me with a soft thunk. No clambering into the torn plastic seat. I studied the dashboard. It even had air conditioning and a CD player.

"Can we listen to music, Dad?" I asked.

Dad laughed and reached toward the radio.

"What's so funny?" I asked, still smiling, waiting for him to explain the joke. If there's one thing about Dad, I have to admit he makes me laugh. Granted, sometimes you're laughing *at* him rather than with him, but I do like his sense of humor, and he has such a funny laugh that you just want to join in.

"You are," Dad said, smiling. He switched the radio on. I looked at the display. NPR!

"Why?"

"Listen to music," he chuckled, as though listening to music was ridiculous or illegal or something.

"But—"

"Shush now, it's the stock market report in a minute." And with that, he turned the radio up and listened attentively while the broadcaster went on about the NASDAQ and foreign exchange rates and all sorts of other things that might as well have been another language to me. I pulled out Charlotte's letter instead.

To my bestest, bestest friend in the whole world,
*   We only just got here, but I wanted to write straightaway. I'm in my new bedroom surrounded by about fifty thousand boxes. I can't find anything. I start my new school tomorrow!*
*   This weekend, we're going to the ASPCA to see if they have any puppies. I can't wait!*

Wish you were here. Miss you so much already.
Write soooooooooon!
Your best friend always,
Charlotte xoxoxoxoxoxoxoxoxoxoxo

I grinned to myself as I folded the letter and put it in my pocket. This was officially the best day ever — and it had hardly even started!

We arrived at the school gates. This was it. The big test. What was he going to do?

"Bye, Dad," I said, leaning over to give him a hug. He flinched and looked at me strangely, as though I'd done something abnormal. Then he gave me an awkward pat on my back, shushed me again, turned the radio up, and shooed me out of the car.

"See you later," I called from the pavement, but he was already whizzing into a three-point turn and zooming off down the road.

Oh. Well, that was weird. I stood on the pavement for a moment, watching the Mustang drive around the corner. Maybe he was going to wave to me at the end of the road.

But he didn't.

I joined the steady stream of kids heading toward

the front door and laughed at myself. Imagine being disappointed that he didn't wave. Having to turn at the door and wave back had driven me crazy nearly every day for years! I would never have to do that again. Yay!

I'd turned up at school in a normal car. And lots of other kids saw me. Things were looking up. No more Hokey Pokey, no frantic waving — and no worries about Dad coming into my class in his pajamas!

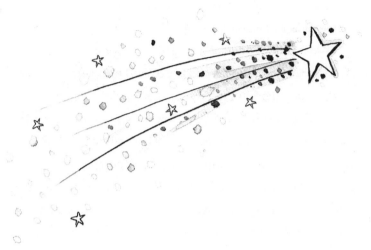

I stood by the stream, waiting for Ray. The grass was wet with dew. I let it soak into my bare feet, filling me up. I closed my eyes, drinking the relief of it into my whole body.

I stretched my wings, opening them all the way out with a quick glance to check that I couldn't be seen.

This little spot was perfect. Trees shielded it in every direction.

The morning was cool. I could hear a few birds tweeting high up in the trees.

After a few moments, I felt one of the sun's rays beam brightly down in front of me, landing in the center of the glade.

"Ray." I smiled, opening my eyes.

He didn't smile back.

"What is it?" I asked. "Is something wrong?"

Ray frowned. The light flickered and broke up for a second, casting shadows in tiny spots around the glade.

"ATC are concerned," he said. "We're not sure that you're giving this assignment your best attention. This isn't the same as your training exercises, you know."

"What do you mean?" I sputtered. "I've already achieved all of the preliminary stages: Making Contact, Establishing Relationship with Client, Imparting Wishes—she's even used the first one already! How can you say I'm not giving the assignment my best attention?"

Ray paused again. "You have done all of these things; it's true. We're not doubting your ability to perform."

"What *are* you doubting, then?" I snapped, leaning back and folding my arms. The dew on my feet felt clammy and cold, and the trees were silent in the sudden stillness.

Ray leaned toward me, warming me with his brightness. "Daisy, you are working with real humans now. Your assignment has tasks within it."

"I know. Like I said, she's already had her first wish!"

"Not just the wishes, Daisy. Extra tasks."

"What do you mean?"

"Lessons. For you. Every assignment has them. When

you pass these, you progress in your development as a fairy godmother. I wasn't sure you were ready for this, and—"

"I *am* ready!" I burst out.

"Daisy, you will have to work harder to prove this."

"How can I work harder? I did the first wish at the earliest shooting star."

"It's not just about efficiency," Ray said with a smile that made the grass light up and sparkle.

"I don't understand."

"Just remember to think as broadly as you can with each wish. Be sure to give Philippa what she really wants."

"I am giving her what she wants!" I said, growing more exasperated by the second. "Haven't you noticed her new parents?"

Ray paused again. "Get to know her, Daisy. And get to know yourself," he said enigmatically before waving and flickering. He was starting to break up. "Oh, and Daisy, you're lucky that you've got me as your supervisor on this assignment."

"Why's that?"

"Breaking Fairy Godmother Code? Revealing your true identity?"

I lowered my head. "I'm sorry. She just—"

"I know. She made you angry. I've persuaded ATC to let you off with a warning on this occasion. But Daisy, learn.

Think about your personal tasks. Do your best. And remember, try to get to know Philippa."

Then he disappeared into a narrow shaft of light and was gone.

I strode away from the glade, angrily shaking leaves off my feet. Work harder, indeed! What was I already doing? I'd granted her the wishes. I'd given her new parents, like she'd asked. I'd showed up at her silly school to make sure that I fulfilled the Monitor and Support part of the assignment. What more did they want?

By the time I arrived at school, I was seething. I got there just before the bell and spotted Philippa in the playground. Lauren and Beth were with her. Trisha Miles was approaching the group just in front of me. She was heading for Philippa and was bound to make some snarky comment as usual.

I sauntered over, almost hoping I wouldn't get there in time to stop Trisha. It wasn't my fault if I was a butterfly beat too late, was it? It would be *so* satisfying to see someone really go at Philippa. I'd never get away with it myself, but boy did I want to now! First she threw me out a window, then she landed me in trouble with ATC.

Get to know her? As if I was interested in doing *that*!

N ice car," Trisha said as she passed me. Nice car! That's what she said! To *me*!

She'd walked away by the time I managed to recover enough to think of a reply. "Thanks," I said weakly to her retreating back. I was still smiling to myself when Daisy appeared by my side.

"What are you looking so happy about?" she asked grumpily.

"Trisha Miles just said something amazing," I replied.

"Really?" She raised an eyebrow. "What did she say?"

"Nice car."

Daisy stared at me. "That's it?"

I nodded. "I know it doesn't sound like much, but it's the nicest thing she's ever said to me!"

Daisy let out her breath in a low whistle. She seemed disappointed. She could at least *pretend* to be happy for me, couldn't she? "I take it you're pleased with your first wish, then?" she said flatly.

I smiled. "Totally. Thank you so much!"

Daisy shrugged. "All in a night's work," she said. We were at the front door. Daisy looked at me for a second, struggling to say something, then shook her head and went inside. I followed her into school.

I couldn't stop smiling all morning. Everything felt different. I know it was a simple thing for Daisy to do, but it meant so much to me. I would never have to worry about my parents embarrassing me again. I couldn't concentrate on anything we did in class; I was too busy thinking about all the things that would be different. No ridiculous van, no more worrying about what my dad might say in front of people, no — my smile fell for a second. No more magic tricks? Would he remember how to make a penny disappear and then reappear in my ear?

I shook myself. It was a small sacrifice — and well worth it for how much better my life was going to be. All that was missing now was sharing it all with Charlotte.

I didn't care if she laughed; I was going to tell her. I would burst if I didn't. Still smiling, I opened my notebook and started scribbling her a letter.

I was packing up at the end of the day when Miss Holdsworth clapped her hands to get our attention. "Children, don't forget to pick up the letter for your parents on your way out. There's a pile by the door."

I grabbed a letter and put it in my bag. A shot of nerves spiked through me as I went out into the playground. I wasn't sure what to expect out there. Maybe the wish wouldn't have worked properly or might have worn off by now. Perhaps I'd even imagined the whole thing and it would be back to normal. Daisy had shot out the door without even saying good-bye, so I couldn't ask her anything. Not that I would have wanted to, anyway. She hadn't been overly forthcoming with reassurance for me so far.

I needn't have worried. There was no van to be seen. I let out a breath that I realized I'd been holding since I came outside.

Mom was standing on the pavement near the Mustang. I smiled when I saw the car. It was so *normal*! So un-vanlike. So not yellow.

She was chatting to some other moms when I went over. She glanced up and gave me a quick smile, then carried on talking.

"Well, it's just not good enough, really, is it?" she was saying. "I mean, they're not babies. It'll be high school soon, and then before you know it, they'll be off to college. There's no point in having them leave here unprepared, is there?"

"Absolutely not," Caroline Hastings's mom said. I didn't really know Caroline all that well. She was in a group who sat on the other side of the class from mine. They were all too trendy, brainy, and hardworking for me: Caroline, Robert, Max, and Vanessa. They weren't unfriendly or weird or anything. They just kept to themselves and seemed to spend hours on end doing homework or discussing when they were next going to their time-share apartments and their villas in France. Just not my kind of kids. And the parents were nothing like mine! Or at least, they never used to be.

"I was talking to the principal just last week," Mrs. Hastings went on. "And he said he was perfectly happy with the amount of homework the children were getting. If you ask me, he was just avoiding the issue. Laziness — that's the problem with these teachers nowadays. They just can't be bothered."

Mom hitched her designer handbag higher up on her shoulder. I stared at it. Mom usually carts everything around in a nasty old recycled bag with SHOP LOCAL written on the side under a picture of a pumpkin. "Well, I have a good mind to say something to Miss Holdsworth myself," she said. "They need more homework; it's as simple as that. I don't want my Philippa starting St. Anne's at a disadvantage."

St. Anne's? The private school on the other side of town? Why was she talking about St. Anne's? I was going to Walchester High!

"Miss Holdsworth has probably gone home now," I said quickly, just in case Mom was planning to march in there right away.

"Philippa, sweetie, don't interrupt while we're talking," Mom said with a quick smile. My cheeks burned up on the spot. Mom *never* scolded me! And in front of other people, too! I stood stiff and still, praying we could get away soon.

Caroline came over then, and Mrs. Hastings turned to get her car keys out of her bag. "Let's discuss it further. We need a plan."

Mom took an electronic planner out of her bag. I stared at that as well. It looked almost as high-tech as Daisy's MagiCell. Mom is the most scatter-brained person in the world — or the second most. Dad's worse. She does buy a planner each year, but she's usually lost it by the end of January and spends the rest of the year writing herself notes on scraps of paper that are lost almost as soon as she's written them.

I looked over her shoulder as she pressed buttons and scrolled through the dates. Arrangements and appointments were crammed into virtually every space. "Let's do dinner. How about coming over on Friday?" Mom said.

"Can't do Friday. Bridge night. Tomorrow?"

"Perfect!" Mom smiled. "Eight at my place?"

"Sounds fab. We can prepare the battle plan," Mrs. Hastings said with a laugh, and they both entered the date into their fancy gadgets.

Battle plan? High-tech planners? Dinner? This was *not* the mom I knew.

"So what's this about St. Anne's?" I asked as casually as I could as we got into the car.

Mom checked and reapplied her lipstick in the mirror before answering. The lipstick that I had never seen her wear in her entire life. In fact, I'd never seen her wear any makeup at all.

"What about it?" she asked, putting the lipstick away and starting the car.

"About me going there?"

Mom laughed. "What *about* you going there, darling? Really, you're talking in riddles today. Are you feeling all right, sweetheart?"

"So I'm going to St. Anne's?" I asked nervously. I couldn't be! I mean, Mom has always hated it. Not just the school itself, the whole idea of private education. The way she talks about private schools and private hospitals, you'd think they were the biggest form of evil that had ever plagued the earth. (After factory farming. And nuclear weapons.)

"Sweetheart, where else would you be going?"

"Walchester High?" I said tentatively.

Mom burst out laughing. "Oh, Philippa, you do make me laugh sometimes," she said. Then she flicked on the radio and listened to a boring talk-radio program all the way home. I didn't dare say anything else. I couldn't risk hearing any more awful news.

St. Anne's! *No one* I knew was going there. It was bad enough that Charlotte had moved away, but at least Lauren and Beth and most of the rest of my class were going to same high school. Now I'd be starting a brand-new school on the other side of town, and the only kids I knew who were going there were the bratty, brainy ones. *And* they had horrible uniforms. You had to wear berets and blazers with a stupid coat of arms on them.

For the first time since I'd made the wish, I seriously began to wonder if I'd done the right thing.

Until dinnertime!

Dinner was the most amazing meal I'd ever eaten — or at least, it was the most amazing thing Mom had ever cooked. You really had to have experienced Mom's cooking to know how bad a meal can get. Not this one. Roast chicken, potatoes, loads of gravy, and chocolate mousse for dessert!

"That was absolutely *delicious!*" I said as I wiped my mouth.

Mom smiled. "Thanks, sweetheart. It was no different from usual, though."

"No different from usual?" I burst out. "It was about as different from usual as you could get!"

Then I realized what I'd said.

"I mean—it was different from other people's usual cooking," I added quickly. "From what normal people eat. That is—other normal people. Like you. Because you're normal, of course. Obviously."

Mom stared at me.

I took a breath and started again. "All I'm trying to say is that it was a delicious meal. Thank you." Then I shut my mouth and wished I hadn't opened it in the first place.

Mom smiled at Dad. He had the paper in front of him again. He had hardly spoken all the way through dinner. That was another thing that was unheard of. Dad usually talked constantly through meals, or insisted that we play games while we eat. Now he was glued to the financial pages again.

"Look at our daughter," Mom said. "So polite, so good."

Dad glanced up from his paper. "Of course she is," he said with a quick smile. "That's how we've raised her."

I was too embarrassed to listen to them talking about me like that, so I got up and took my plate to the sink. I started rinsing it. Dad and I usually cleaned up together.

"What are you doing?" Mom asked.

"Cleaning up."

"Put them in the dishwasher, silly," she said with a laugh.

Dishwasher? Since when did we have a dishwasher? Mom always said they were a criminal waste of electricity. I opened a cabinet under the sink. Not there; just a trash can. Another door next to it. Washing machine.

Dad got up and opened the door on the other side of the sink. Dishwasher. He put his plate inside as though that was what we did everyday.

"Right, I'd better get going," he said, giving Mom a quick kiss on the forehead. "Don't wait up, sweetheart. Not sure when I'll be back."

"Do you really have to go out again?" Mom

asked. "We haven't had a night in together for nearly a week."

"Come on, darling, it's important that I turn up for squash. You know all the deals get done on the court."

"Or in the bar afterward," Mom sniped.

"Darling, it's for you I do it. For all of us. It's not just fun, you know."

Mom squeezed her lips tightly together, but she didn't reply.

"See ya, kid," Dad added as he passed me. And with that, he was gone.

Mom brought her plate over. "I'll take care of this," she said with a sigh. "You can go and get started on your homework."

"It's OK. I'll help," I said. I cleared the table while she filled the dishwasher. We didn't talk as we worked. I didn't know what to say to her, this strange, distant woman, my mom.

Later in my bedroom, I unpacked my bag to get started on my homework, and the letter from school fell out. I stole a quick look. It was all about a talent show at school next week. The prize was a choice of vacations for the whole family. I tried to imagine going away with my family. Where would we go?

In the old days, we'd have gone camping and made our own entertainment with songs and jokes and conversation. I couldn't imagine my new mom and dad doing that. They'd probably want to stay at a five-star hotel with Jacuzzis and pools and tennis courts.

Well, that didn't sound too bad, either. Not that we'd win the prize. Talent show! There was one small problem with that: the word *talent*. And the fact that I didn't have any. Plus the fact that I could never stand up in front of a big group. Not again. Sometimes I wished I could. Would I ever be able to do it again? I couldn't imagine it. I could never risk the humiliation of what had happened last time. The very last time I helped at a party.

I couldn't even think about it.

I stuffed the letter back in my bag and got out my math homework.

But I couldn't concentrate. It was too hard, anyway. I've always preferred words to numbers. Charlotte was much better than me at math, and she used to help explain things to me. We'd always done our homework together.

I considered going up to the tree house and asking Daisy. But she wouldn't want to help me. I didn't even know if she was good at math. I didn't really know anything about her. In fact, the more I thought about it, the more I realized I didn't know anything about *anyone* anymore. Mom and Dad were practically as strange to me as Daisy. Charlotte was hundreds of miles away. Nothing made sense in the normal way.

I shut my math book and grabbed my magic book instead. Anything to take my mind off the strange and unfamiliar reality of my world.

Things looked better in the morning. They smelled better, for a start. Bacon and eggs. Is there a more perfect way to start your day than bacon and eggs?

I shook off the previous night's miserable mood and got ready for school. As soon as I'd finished breakfast, I ran down the road to mail my letter to Charlotte. I'd finished it last night. I told her everything — I'd just have to wait and see whether or not she believed me.

I was ready to jump in the car as soon as Dad called me. I didn't even mind him listening to the radio. It gave me a chance to look out the window and think about the day ahead. The day that wasn't going to start with anyone embarrassing me. Bliss.

For the second day in a row, I arrived at school smiling.

"Hey, what do you think about the talent show?" Lauren whispered across the table as Miss Holdsworth took attendance.

I shrugged. I didn't particularly think *anything* of it.

"Beth and I are going to enter," she said, beaming with pride at her best friend.

"Really?" I couldn't keep the shock out of my voice. Beth and Lauren were about as exceptionally talented as me, as far as I knew. "What are you going to do?"

"Sing!"

"Not on our own," Beth said. "A few of us from choir are going to do a couple of songs."

"Really? That's great," I said.

"What about you? Why don't you enter?"

"And do what?" I asked.

"You three, are you paying attention?" Miss Holdsworth asked.

"Sorry, Miss Holdsworth," we replied in unison. I was glad she'd stopped the conversation before we'd gotten around to discussing in detail how untalented and uninteresting I was.

Daisy burst through the door. "Sorry I'm late," she said, panting. "I overslept."

Her uniform was all askew, her shirt untucked, and her sweater loosely tied around her waist. She yanked her sweater on as soon as she sat down, but not before I'd seen the bulge under the back. It looked as though her shoulder blades were about twice the normal size. I wasn't the only one to spot it, either. Trisha Miles and the others at her table were all pointing at Daisy and whispering to one another by the time she sat down.

Miss Holdsworth nodded briskly and ticked her name off on the list. "I'll let it go just this once, since you're new," she said. "Try not to do it again."

Daisy looked across at Trisha and her gang as she pulled up the chair next to me. They were still pointing at her and giggling behind their hands.

I wanted to say something comforting to her. I wanted her to know that it wasn't just her, that those girls laugh at anyone, given half a chance. Daisy just gave me a sharp look and stared down at her books. Her face was absolutely purple, though.

"What?" I asked, wondering why *I* was the one getting dirty looks.

"I tossed and turned all night in that place," she snapped. "I only got to sleep at about five this morning."

"How's that my fault?" I whispered.

"I didn't say it was, did I?" Daisy whispered back.

I rolled my eyes.

"Look, I know it's not your fault," she went on. "But do you think you could sneak me out a blanket? I'm not used to sleeping on hard, wooden floors."

I nodded. "I'll see what I can do." Then I opened my notebook and tried to concentrate on the lesson without getting too annoyed by Daisy moaning and groaning her way through everything we did.

As the day went on, I kept thinking about my first wish and wondering if I'd really made the best use of it. I mean, OK, Dad had been really embarrassing and made me feel like I stood out in front of my friends sometimes. And Mom could be a bit of a pain. But had they honestly been all that bad? And had changing them really made a major difference in my life? Was I truly any happier now?

Mom was chatting with her new friends again when I got out of school. "See you tonight," she called over her shoulder to them as we got in the car. By the time we were halfway home, it occurred to me that she hadn't even asked how my day had been. Mind you, I hadn't asked about hers, either. The more I thought about it, the more I felt dumbstruck. I didn't know what to say to my own mom.

I went straight to my room when we got back. I was lying on my bed, reading "How to Snake-Charm a Pencil," when there was a knock on my door.

Mom's face poked in. "Sweetheart, shouldn't you be doing your homework?" she asked.

"I'll do it in a minute. Just want to finish reading this trick."

"I'd rather you did it now," Mom said firmly.

I closed the book. Mom had never nagged me about homework before. And I'd never turned anything in late. Why the big fuss? I wanted to say something, but it all felt pointless. "OK," I said instead. But there were some strange feelings bubbling and curdling around in my stomach. Anger. Injustice. Frustration. It just wasn't fair!

"And I'd like you to make yourself scarce when Mrs. Hastings comes over later. We've got some private matters to discuss. I'll make your dinner earlier, all right?"

"What about Dad?" I asked.

"What about him?"

"Will he eat with me?"

"Don't be silly, darling. Your father will be at the office. You know it's his late night tonight."

"But he was out last night, too."

"He's a busy man. And a successful one, too. Would you rather he was at home all the time and we couldn't afford to buy decent food?"

I was about to answer. *Yes, I would, actually!* I wanted to say. *I would rather he was home! I don't care where you get our dinner from; I'd just like to feel that we're a family again. I want my dad bounding around doing magic tricks; I want you to be interested in me, not just plot my education with the snobby moms. I even want . . .*

My thoughts stopped dead. When they started again, I was shocked to discover what they were. *I even want our stupid, old, bright-yellow VW van back, and I don't care if Dad embarrasses me on the way to school. At least you both cared about me before. At least you noticed me.*

"No, of course not, Mom," I said, instead of any of that. "Sorry." I put my magic book down and got out my homework.

"There's a good girl," Mom said with another of those tight smiles. "Dinner will be ready in an hour," she added as she closed the door behind her.

As soon as she'd gone, I shut my schoolbooks. I didn't even have much homework to do. What was the big deal about homework, anyway? What happened to dancing around the kitchen and pulling pennies out of my ear and thinking that spending the evening talking to one another and playing games were more important than cleaning up or working?

For the twenty billionth time since Charlotte had left, I wished I had a friend I could talk to. Or even just the company of someone my own age. I remembered Daisy asking if I could bring her a blanket. I knew it was unlikely that I'd get any sympathy from Daisy, but at least if I went to see her, it would be someone to talk to. Maybe she'd understand. Maybe she could do something to make the wish work a bit better. It had to be worth a try. Anything would be better than feeling like this.

I pulled a blanket out from the closet in the hallway and grabbed a couple of textbooks. "I'm going to work in the tree house," I said as I went through the kitchen. "Just taking the blanket to make it more comfy. Is that OK?"

"I don't know what you see in that tree house," Mom said. "It's about time we tore it down and did something useful with the yard."

I tried not to let Mom's words get to me. She didn't mean it. They wouldn't tear down the tree house. Surely they wouldn't.

Too miserable to reply, I set off down the backyard, praying that Daisy could think of something, anything, to stop my life from feeling like it had gone from bad to terrible!

"Daisy?" I pulled myself up through the trapdoor.

She was sitting on the floor, punching buttons on her MagiCell and writing notes on some paper from a notebook of mine. She looked up when she saw me.

"About time," she said, reaching out for the blanket. "Is this the best you could do?"

I took a deep breath before replying. *Don't let her get to you. Just don't.* "Yes," I said firmly. "It's the best I could do. Why? Isn't it good enough for you?"

Daisy sniffed. "It's hardly better than the floor. You might as well have not bothered."

Suddenly, it was all too much. Something snapped inside me. I threw the blanket down. "Well, in that case, I'm sorry I did!" I snapped. "I'm sorry I bothered bringing you a blanket, and I'm sorry I made that stupid wish! I'm sorry I ever laid *eyes* on you!"

Daisy looked up at me. We stared at each other in silence. I could feel my hands shaking by my sides. I'd never spoken my mind so strongly in my life!

"*You're* sorry you ever laid eyes on *me*?" Daisy said very slowly and deliberately. "*You're* sorry? Ha!" She stood up so we were facing each other, staring hard into each other's eyes. "Believe me, you're not half as sorry as I am!"

"Why do you hate me so much?" I said, wishing my eyes would behave. *Don't cry. Don't you dare cry,* I ordered them.

"Do you think I'm going to like you after what you did? Throwing me out of a window!"

"Oh, for goodness' sake, not that again!"

"Not that again?" Daisy sneered. "It might not be a big deal for *you* to do something so violent and cruel, but where *I'm* standing, it's pretty major stuff. And you got me into trouble with my supervisor, too."

"It was an ACCIDENT!" I yelled. Our voices were growing louder and louder every time one of us spoke. I could just imagine Mom coming outside any minute now and hearing us. That was the last thing I needed. "It was an accident," I repeated, more softly. "I never meant to hurt you. I never meant to harm you at all."

"Don't lie!" Daisy retorted. "You knew what I was. Don't try to deny it. You knew I was a fairy, you knew I was going to come alive at midnight, and you still threw me out of a window. How could that not harm me?"

I didn't have a reply. All I knew was that a few days ago, I had a best friend, a pair of loving — if slightly nutty — parents, and the promise of a fairy of my own. Now, every bit of everything had gone wrong. I had nothing and no one. I'd never felt so alone in my life.

"I'll get you another blanket as soon as I can," I said, and then I climbed down and walked miserably back to the house.

I paced around the glade more furiously than ever. They'd called me to yet another meeting! How *dare* they! And how dare *she*! She should be thankful for me! The ungrateful little . . .

And those stupid girls at school. Imagine laughing at me like that. Laughing at *me*! Like I was one of the silly children. As though I really belonged at that table with Philippa and her geeky friends! I'd show them. I'd show all of them! I'd had a hard enough job proving to ATC that I was ready to work solo. I didn't need some stupid human girls trying to put me down!

I would have some stern words for Ray when he got here.

A sharp ray of sun pierced the glade, lighting up the leaves in bright green strips. Even the trees seemed to stand taller.

"What is the meaning of this?" Ray asked.

"Of what?" I said as innocently and politely as I could. I'd never seen him look angry like this, and it made me think I should tread more carefully than last time. "I haven't done anything—have I?"

"No. You haven't done anything at all since your last meeting. You haven't behaved any differently toward Philippa. In fact, if anything, your conduct has been even worse. What exactly are you playing at?"

"I'm not playing at anything," I countered. "I'm not playing at *all*. It's work. Not play."

"And that is the root of your problem," he snapped, his beam growing sharper, almost blinding me. Even the ground felt brittle and hard in his glare.

"The root of my problem? I don't understand."

"Exactly. You don't understand. We haven't managed to get through to you yet, have we?" he said. "I told ATC I didn't think you were ready for this assignment, and you are proving me more right by the moment."

"I was ready!" I said. "I *am* ready! Look how well I did in training. I'm more than ready for 3WD. I know the procedures like the back of my hand!"

"Procedures!" Ray shook his head. "Daisy," he said. "Hold out your hand."

"What?"

"Hold it out."

I put my hand out, palm facing up.

"Other way."

I turned my hand over.

"Now look at it. Look at the back of your hand."

Feeling only slightly stupid, I studied the back of my hand. Five fingers, pale, a little dry. I'd have to get some new Fairyskin hand-care cream to deal with—

"How do you feel about what you see?" he asked me.

"How do I *feel* about it?" I asked. "About the back of my hand?"

"Yes, Daisy. How do you feel about it?"

"I don't *feel* anything about it! It's my hand. It's not something I have great emotion for!"

He nodded sharply, throwing alternating light and shadow on the willow. "Exactly. Thank you; you can put your hand down now. You have illustrated my point perfectly."

I looked again at my hand. Huh? I'd illustrated his point? How could I have done that when I didn't even understand what his point was?

"I'm contacting FGR," he said.

Fairy Godmother Replacement! Why was he contacting them?

"You can pack your things. We'll take you back to ATC tonight."

"Take me back? What do you mean? What's going on?"

"I'm taking you off the case," he said simply. Then he started to fade.

"WAIT!" I yelled. The beam flickered back into life. As it did, I became aware of how weary I was. The life cycle was taking it out of me. "Please," I said, feeling weak and pathetic.

"Daisy, it isn't working. We thought you would be up to the challenge and the tasks of this assignment, but we made a mistake. It happens."

"What do you mean, the challenge and the tasks? I'm easily up to it! I'll prove it."

"We've been wanting you to learn something. Some of the others thought you were ready, but we were too hasty. You're not ready. I want you to take a new case."

His words didn't make any sense to me. Of course I was up to this assignment. It was easy! I didn't know what they wanted me to learn, or what he was talking about—but I didn't even care about that.

All I knew was that I didn't want to be taken off the case. I didn't really know why; I couldn't explain. Whatever my reason, it was just out of my reach. I just really, really didn't want to be taken off the case.

"Please," I said again. "Don't take me off it. Let me try again. Tell me what you want me to learn, and I'll do it. I'll learn it ten times over if you like. Just let me stay on this case."

"Why?" he asked.

Philippa's face came into my mind. What was I doing, thinking about her? But even as I questioned myself, I knew the answer. I felt bad, and I suddenly realized I wanted to make things right.

I thought about how angry she'd been last night when she came to see me. It wasn't her fault if the blanket wasn't thick enough. She'd tried her best. It wasn't even her fault that she'd thrown me out of the window. She was scared. I could see that now. I could see lots of things. Mostly what I could see was Philippa's sad face, the look in her eyes that showed the hope that maybe I could do something to make her happier. That maybe I could even have been her friend.

"Just let me try again," I said.

"Why? So you can show off about your results and the speediness of your wish control? I'm sorry, but it's—"

"No!" I shouted. And before I could stop myself, or even think about what I was saying, I added, "Not because of that! Because of Philippa. Because I haven't said good-bye. Because we had an argument and I didn't say I'm sorry. Because I want to see if I can make her happy again. OK?"

Ray looked at me for a long time. Then, finally, he smiled. His beam grew broader and warmer for a split second. "OK," he said, nodding gently. "Take the day off. Have a rest. Remember the life cycle. You don't have long. Plenty of water. Give all of this some thought. Back on duty this evening."

"Thank you," I breathed, sagging with a relief that I couldn't understand.

I sat down on the grass for a while after he'd gone. Not just because of the growing exhaustion of the life cycle. It was something else, too. Something about the conversation had shaken me—and I still didn't understand what it was.

chapter nine

RECONCILIATION

I busied myself, pretending to sharpen my pencil by the door while Miss Holdsworth took attendance. Really, I just wanted to be able to look out for Daisy. Where was she?

She'd been late each morning so far, but she was usually here by the time Miss Holdsworth finished attendance. Not today, though.

"Philippa, any sign of your friend?" Miss Holdsworth asked me as she handed the attendance sheet to Paul Simmons to take down to the office. I followed him down the corridor with my eyes, just in case Daisy bumped into him on her way in.

"My friend?" I asked. Had she just called Daisy my friend? She had to have walked around school with her eyes closed all week to think Daisy was my friend.

"I use the term loosely," Miss Holdsworth said with that sarcastic edge that teachers must learn at college; they all seem to use it. "Daisy French."

I silenced an urge to correct her. Daisy had already told me she just used the first word she'd seen on my books to make up her surname.

"I'm sure she'll be here soon," I said, blowing on my pencil. "She probably got held up by something."

"Yes," said Miss Holdworth frowning. "She's obviously been held up by *something*. I would like it if she managed to get to school on time perhaps once in her first week. And you're responsible for her, Philippa, so could you please ensure that she invests in an alarm clock, or at the very least a watch, before the end of the week?"

"Yes, Miss Holdsworth," I said, returning to my seat.

Lauren and Beth shot me sympathetic looks all the way through first period. I didn't want their sympathy. I didn't really want anything from anyone. I could hardly believe I was thinking this, but for the first time all week, I didn't even want Charlotte. I just wanted Daisy to turn up.

I'd been so mean and horrible to her. What had possessed me to talk to her like that? I *never* spoke that way to people. I shouldn't have done it. It was totally uncalled for, and now look what had happened—she hadn't even come to school. That's how upset she'd been. That's how stupid it is to lose your temper with someone.

If anything had happened to her, I'd never forgive myself. Not just because she was my fairy godmother and had another two wishes to grant me. That wasn't even the main thing. I just needed to know she was all right. I don't know why I cared so much. It wasn't as if she cared about *me*. She'd made that plain enough. But that was no reason to be nasty or to shout like I had last night.

I needed to apologize to her; it was as simple as that.

By lunchtime, I'd had enough of sitting around waiting. I'd decided. I was going to find her.

I glanced around to check that no one was watching before sneaking out of the playground. I ran to the end of the road and was about to cross it when I noticed a bus heading toward me. It wouldn't get me all the way home, but it was better than walking. I dashed to the bus stop and climbed aboard, praying no one had noticed me.

All the way home, I thought about Daisy and about how everything had gone so wrong. It wasn't her fault, though. She was just doing her job. She gave me the wish I'd asked for. If it was anyone's stupid fault, it was my own. I *had* to apologize to her. She *had* to forgive me.

Fifteen minutes later, I was running down the last few streets to get home. We had an hour and a half for lunch on Fridays, so I figured I had about forty-five minutes before I needed to get back to school.

I ran upstairs to my room, looking all around to see if there was any sign she'd been there. Nothing. I glanced briefly at the daisy in the eggcup. Its head drooped low, and a couple of petals had dropped onto the floor.

I dumped my bag and ran down to the tree house.

"Daisy!" I shouted breathlessly from the bottom of the ladder. No reply. I clambered up the steps. "Daisy, are you here?"

But it was empty. The blanket lay crumpled on the floor, where she must have slept on it last night. I winced as I remembered telling her that I'd see if I could find anything better. I hadn't even done that. I was such a bad person — it was no wonder Daisy didn't like me and my parents had no time for me.

I slumped on the floor of the tree house.

Absentmindedly, I picked up a few coins from among the dust. They'd been inside the box that we'd put the wish vouchers in. I practiced some magic tricks, holding the coins out, then closing my hands, flicking my wrists and making them disappear. I made them reappear from underneath the blanket, then shook my wrists again, and they'd disappear. Lost in the magic trick, I felt my mood lighten. I practiced more tricks, trying fancier and more elaborate ways of making the coins disappear and reappear, flicking my wrists around, swirling my hands in the air, above my head, behind my back, spinning around and finding the coins on the window ledge —

"Philippa!"

I spun around. Daisy was at the top of the ladder, dragging herself up through the trapdoor. She looked tired. Her eyes were dark, and her hair was flat and lank. She reminded me of the daisy in my bedroom. Drooping in a similar way. The life cycle was marching on for them both.

"Daisy!" My face broke into a grin. I just barely stopped myself from running over and hugging her.

Daisy was smiling at me, too. I realized I'd never seen her smile before. It made her whole face change. Normally, her face had a kind of pointy look about it, with her sharp little nose and tiny chin and eyes that seemed to be squinting and narrowed all the time. When she smiled, it was as if her face softened and became rounder, and a light turned on behind her eyes.

"Where were you?" I asked. "I've been so worried."

"Worried? Why?"

I looked down, ashamed of myself. I could hardly even say the words. I didn't want to remind either of us about how mean I'd been to her.

"The things I said last night," I mumbled eventually. "I was horrible." Staring at my feet, I added in a quiet voice, "I'm really, really sorry."

Daisy didn't say anything for a while. She must

have been furious with me. Well, I didn't blame her. But then I looked through my eyelashes, sneaking a look at her without lifting my head. She was still smiling! "You think *you* were horrible?" she said.

I nodded.

Daisy let out a burst of laughter. "Philippa, if you think *that* was horrible, you should hear *me* on a bad day." Then she was the one to look embarrassed. "Well, you have," she added. "In fact, you've seen me on pretty much the worst days. And it's me who's been horrible to you. You've been really patient with me. You've put up with me being a real rain-cloud and you've still tried to be nice. You even brought me a blanket when I'd been so snappy and nasty with you."

"I know, but look how I lost my temper with you when I brought it."

Daisy laughed again. "You call that losing your temper?"

"Well, yes, it was unnecessary and uncalled for and—"

"Philippa, if that's the most horrible you can be, then you're an even nicer person than I already thought you were . . . than I've only just realized you are."

I stared at her, my mouth trying to twitch up into a smile. I wouldn't let it, though. I must have heard her wrong. Either that or there was a big sting of a punch line on the way in a minute.

"You think I'm a nice person?" I asked timidly, pulling at my sleeves with my fingers while I waited for her to reply.

Daisy gave me the biggest smile yet. "Yes, actually," she said. "I think you're one of the nicest people I've ever met and you wouldn't harm a fly."

Then she stopped herself and coughed. "Well, you wouldn't harm a fly on purpose," she added.

"Oh, Daisy, there's all that, too. I'm so sorry I threw you out the window. I had no idea, I mean, I never would have —"

Daisy stopped me with her hand. "I know," she said. "I realize that now. And Philippa, I'm the one who owes you an apology, not the other way around, OK?"

"You don't owe me anything! You've already given me a wish, and you're going to give me two more," I said. "I mean, that's if I'm still getting them."

"Of course you are. And anyway, that's just my job. That's not about . . ."

Daisy stopped, as though she couldn't find the words she was looking for.

"Not about what?" I nudged gently.

"About, about . . ." Daisy's face reddened. She looked as if she were trying to force a word out of her mouth, but it wouldn't come.

I waited, looking at her encouragingly.

"About caring!" she burst out eventually. Almost angrily. "There, I've said it. I care. I care what happens to you, OK?"

For a moment, the old defiant Daisy was there again, and I wondered if she was going to take it all back. I decided not to say anything. I didn't want to say the wrong thing.

"They were going to take me off the case," she said. "They wanted to replace me."

"Really? You mean I wouldn't have seen you again?"

Daisy nodded. "They said I'm failing some special task. I don't know what it is, and I don't even care! I just had this really weird feeling when they said they were going to take me off the case. It was as though a voice inside me was begging them not to, and I didn't even know whose voice it was, or where it was coming from. It was as if I'd been taken over by someone else! Some real soft-cloud!"

"So what happened?"

"Once I pleaded with them to let me stay on the case, they changed their minds."

I let out a breath. "I'm glad," I said, smiling shyly at her.

She smiled back. "Me, too. I had some time to think today." She pulled at the edges of the blanket while she talked. "I realized that I didn't want to leave without saying I was sorry for being so mean." She paused for a long time. "And I guess I want to see this assignment through and give you some wishes that will make you happier."

Daisy was pulling furiously at the blanket now. I felt as if I had a big air pump inside me, blowing me up till I was big and tight inside. "Thank you," I managed to say eventually.

Daisy shook her head. "No, thank *you*."

"Thank me? What for?"

She shrugged. "Everything. But mostly for last night."

"Last night? You're thanking me for yelling at you?"

Daisy laughed. "Yeah, I guess I am. You helped me see things differently."

"Well, I'll never do that again," I said. "I don't want to be like that."

"Hey, you shouldn't be so hard on yourself. You weren't that bad, you know. You stood up for yourself. There's nothing wrong with doing that sometimes."

I took her words in. I'd stood up for myself. I'd always been so afraid of doing that, of doing anything that made me the center of attention. So worried that the world would collapse around me if I did—that people would hate me, I'd lose them, and everything would go wrong. Well, things had been going wrong enough lately, without me standing up for myself, and it hadn't made things any worse. Maybe the world didn't end when you stood up for yourself.

Still, I didn't want to do it again. There was really no need to be like that.

"You haven't missed much at school today," I said, sensing it was time to change the subject.

Daisy looked relieved. "Didn't think so," she said, pulling her sweater off and settling down on the blanket. I couldn't help staring at her back, how her shoulders stuck out strangely without her sweater on. I knew it was just her wings, but it looked really weird.

Daisy saw me looking.

"I'm sorry about the girls the other day," I said clumsily. "They'll laugh at anyone. It doesn't mean anything."

Daisy waved her hand. "Hey, I'm over it," she said. The catch in her voice told me that she wasn't over it at all. The sudden forced smile told me not to push it.

As she took her books out of her bag, a piece of paper fell out. She opened it.

"Oh, that's the letter we got the other day," I said. "Just ignore it; it's only about a silly talent show next week."

Daisy read the letter. "Hey, you should enter this," she said.

"Yeah, right." I laughed. "Doing what?"

Daisy pointed to my hands. "That thing you were doing when I came in."

"The tricks?"

"It looked fantastic!" she said. "Do you know any others?"

"Yeah, loads, but —"

"You could do them!"

"What, like a magic show?" For a second, I imagined myself onstage, doing my magic, completely lost in the world that it takes me into, hundreds of pairs of eyes staring at me, amazed by my tricks. Hundreds of mouths open in silent awe. Then I thought again. Hundreds of people sitting out there, watching the stage. Me on it. Completely on my own. Standing there in front of the entire school.

My mouth felt as though it had a desert inside it. "No way," I said. "I'd never do that."

"Why not?"

"I just couldn't stand up in front of the whole school like that. I'd die."

Daisy laughed. "You wouldn't die! Come on, what's the worst thing that could happen?"

I knew very well what the worst thing was that could happen. It had already happened, and I was never, ever going to let it happen again.

"What is it, Philippa?" Daisy asked more softly.

I shook my head. I didn't trust myself to speak.

"Hey, there *is* something, isn't there?" Daisy said.

"I've never told anyone," I said eventually.

"Never told anyone what?"

"Why I can't do it."

"Tell me. I'll help you."

I looked up at her. Her eyes were so gentle and sincere. Looking into them, I knew right then that I could trust her. I'd never even told Charlotte. A pang of guilt flashed through me as I realized that I'd hardly thought about Charlotte all day. I shook it off. "Do you promise you won't laugh at me?" I asked.

"Of course I won't laugh."

"And you won't tell anyone?"

"Never."

I took a deep breath. "OK, then," I said. And then I told her what had happened.

"It was years ago," I started. "I used to go along to the parties with Mom and Dad. They always encouraged me to sing for the kids. It was this boy's ninth birthday party. I was six. Mom and Dad always wanted to show me off. They'd tell me I was brilliant at everything; they said I could sing, said I had the voice of an angel. And I was stupid enough to believe them."

I looked up to see Daisy's eyes intent on mine. "Go on," she encouraged me.

"So they got me to sing. Up in the front in my white frilly dress with a pink satin sash. I got about half a verse into the song, and then I heard them all giggling. Just the boys in the back row at first, and I tried to ignore them. I sang a bit louder. Then it spread to the next row, and then the one in front of that, too. Then the whole room was breaking up into hysterical laughter. I glanced over at Mom and Dad, petrified, but they just smiled back at me, waving for me to carry on."

"So what happened?" Daisy asked.

"Somehow I made it to the end of the second

verse. Then I felt something running down my leg. Hot liquid. I couldn't believe it! Right there, right in front of a room full of people laughing at me because I sang like an injured cat, just when things couldn't have been much worse—I'd wet myself!"

I glanced at Daisy to check that she wasn't laughing at me. She wasn't. Cheeks burning, I carried on.

"I pretended I couldn't remember the last verse and quickly whizzed through the chorus again, then I took a quick bow and scampered off the stage. I didn't look back. My leg was wet, and I ran straight to the bathroom. I never found out if it had reached the floor or if anyone knew what had happened. I was never, ever going to ask."

"Did you have to do it again?"

I nodded. "The next week, Mom and Dad said I should sing again. I'd rather have died, but I couldn't tell them why. So I did. Tried to, anyway. It was a girl's seventh birthday party. I stood up there in front of her and her friends."

"What did you do?"

"I just turned to stone. I couldn't sing, couldn't speak, couldn't move. I literally stood there like a statue for about five minutes. Eventually, Mom ran over and grabbed my hand. 'She's a bit shy sometimes,' she said, and pulled me away while the girls started playing a game. They never tried to make me sing after that. And I've never, ever stood up in front of a group of people since then."

Daisy stared at me in silence. My cheeks were burning up. *I shouldn't have told her. She must think I am the biggest baby ever. Why did I tell her?*

"You poor thing," she said, putting her hand on my arm. "That sounds awful."

She wasn't laughing.

"But do you know what?" she said.

"What?"

"We're going to fix it." Then she rummaged in her bag again and took out her MagiCell. "Hang on a minute." She punched a few numbers and studied the screen for a few seconds. "Yes! I thought so!" she said.

"What?"

"Look at that," she said, smiling as she held the MagiCell out to me. In glowing numbers, the screen showed a list of dates and times. The first one was tonight, followed by a few more. Daisy scrolled through them, pointing to the fourth date in the list.

"What's that?" I asked.

"It's next Tuesday. The night before the talent show."

"What's the list?"

Daisy put the MagiCell down. "The list shows the times of all the shooting stars — and there's one on Tuesday night. Don't you see?"

"See what?" I asked. Clearly I didn't see, whatever it was I was meant to be seeing.

"You could make a wish the night before the show."

"How would that help?"

"It's your chance to leave it all behind you. You could wish to have all the confidence in the world. You could wish to banish fear. You could wish to forget about what happened to you back then and know that it will never ever happen again."

I thought about what she said. It was tempting. "I don't know," I said. "I mean, what if it doesn't work?"

"It always works!"

"What if I get all the confidence, but I'm no good

anyway? It wouldn't matter how confident I was if my show was terrible! They'd still laugh at me."

"OK, that's it." Daisy got up and went over to the other side of the tree house.

"Wait, don't go!"

"I'm not going, you silly sun ray." She sat down on the floor across the tree house from me and folded her arms.

"What are you doing, then?"

"I'm your audience," she said with a smile. "Show me what you can do."

"Really?" I asked shyly.

"Really!"

I wanted to. I told myself I'd only be doing it in front of one person, which I'd done loads of times before. And I really had missed showing Charlotte my tricks and seeing her face when I'd impressed her with a new one.

"OK," I said. "Just give me a minute."

I gathered up a few bits and pieces from the floor that I needed, stacking them on the window ledge behind me. The coins, a couple of newspapers, an orange, a pen, and paper.

"Ready?" I asked nervously.

"Absolutely." Daisy smiled.

I picked up the coins. "OK," I said, my voice still trembling a little. "I'll start with these. Which hand is the coin in?"

By the time I'd finished my show, Daisy was clapping so loudly that I thought Mom would hear us and come to see what was going on.

"Philippa, that was amazing!" she said. "That was better magic than I've seen some fairy godmothers do!"

"Really?" I asked, my cheeks on fire.

"You bet!" She stood up and brushed herself off. "You're entering the talent show."

"Oh, but—"

"No buts. There's nothing to worry about. The show is incredible. You'll blow them away. All you have to worry about is the confidence thing. And you can wish for that the night before."

"You're definitely sure about the shooting star on Tuesday?" I asked.

"Positive. MagiCell information is the most precise in the whole sky. It's never been wrong yet."

I drew in a breath, held it for a moment, and then slowly let it out. "OK," I said. My hands shook as much as my voice, but I'd decided. "I'll sign up this afternoon — on one condition."

"What's that?"

"You come back in to school with me."

Daisy grinned as she reached for her bag. "What are we waiting for?"

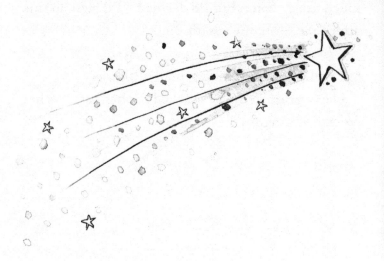

Philippa added her name to the talent-show sign-up sheet as we passed the bulletin board.

"Come on, we've still got fifteen minutes of lunch left," she said. "Let's join the others."

As we sat down in the cafeteria, I happened to glance over at Trisha. She was nudging her friend and whispering something.

Ignore them, ignore them. They don't matter.

I don't know why Trisha suddenly bothered me so much, but she did. Just the way she looked at you made you feel like you weren't good enough—for what, I don't know. Just not good enough to be in her gang, I guess. Which was what everyone wanted to be. I mean, I was really glad

Philippa and I had made up. Things felt so much better now. But still—I didn't really want Trisha to know how friendly Philippa and I were now. I wasn't prepared to be next on her hit list.

So I shifted my chair again and got my books out without saying anything else to Philippa. It wasn't as though I was doing anything mean. I wasn't ignoring her or anything. I just didn't see the need to advertise our newfound friendship to the world.

At lunchtime, we sat with Lauren and Beth. The list had gone up with the talent show entries, and they'd seen Philippa's name on it.

"What are you going to do?" Lauren asked.

Philippa glanced nervously at me.

"It's a surprise," I said with a wink. "But it's fantastic!"

Philippa shot me a grateful smile.

Lauren and Beth tried to guess what it could be. They kept coming up with more and more outrageous suggestions.

"Lion taming!" Beth said.

"Tightrope walking!" Lauren countered. Philippa and I just laughed. I realized that I hadn't done much laughing since I'd started the assignment. It felt good. Beth started joking about how much water I drank. I couldn't exactly explain it was because I became like a wilting flower if I didn't get enough water! Philippa made a joke out of that, too, so I didn't have to reply. It was as though we totally understood each other, as though we could read each other's minds and finish each other's thoughts. I realized I hadn't felt so relaxed and happy in a really long time. Maybe ever.

And then Trisha came in.

"Hey, it's the freaks and geeks!" she said loudly, nudging her friend. "Mind if we join you?"

The four of us fell silent as Trisha and Jacqui shoved into us and sat down.

"Hey, Jacqui," Trisha said loudly. "Do you think we're *talented* enough to sit at this table?"

My skin turned cold. *Don't let them get to you. Don't, don't, don't!*

"Or is it only skinny little girls and weirdo math geeks and freaks with sticky-out shoulders who can sit here?"

The pair of them burst out laughing. And that was it. Freaks! They'd called me a freak! I couldn't let them get away with it. Suddenly, I forgot about all the laughing we'd been doing. I forgot about how well Philippa and I had been getting along. I couldn't see any of it through the red mist of anger that was rolling into a ball inside me.

"Ignore them," Philippa whispered. "They do this to everyone. Just keep quiet and they'll get bored and leave us alone soon."

And then I did something I hate myself for.

I shifted away from Philippa. If she wanted to sit quietly and be on the receiving end of Trisha's jokes, that was up to her. But I wasn't going to join her there. And before I knew it, my anger-ball had gathered Philippa up, too. Why couldn't she stand up to Trisha for once—like she did with me the other day? Why did she have to be so weak? In that moment, I was just as angry with her as I was with Trisha.

"Seems the freaks and geeks have been struck dumb," Jacqui sneered.

"Bunch of wimps, all of them," Trisha replied. With that, she started to get up from her seat.

I reached right across Philippa to grab Trisha's arm, pulling her back down in her seat. "Who do you think you're talking to?" I growled.

Philippa and the others seemed to shrink in their chairs. Even that annoyed me. They were being exactly what Trisha said—a bunch of wimps.

"You think I'm like *them*?" I said, my anger snatching away the loyalty I'd been so happy to feel only moments earlier. I couldn't stop myself. I wasn't having Trisha Miles think that she was better than me—or associate me with girls she despised.

"You think I'd hang out with them, given a choice?" I said, my brain taking a leave of absence as my fury took charge. "Think I'm not good enough to be in your gang? Well, I've got news for you. I'm way better than them— and you know what? I'm way better than you, too!"

Trisha looked at me for a moment. Then she looked at Jacqui and burst out laughing. "Yeah, whatever—freak!" she said. Then the pair of them got up from their seats and walked off, laughing and throwing their heads back.

Philippa looked at me in silence. Her eyes were shining and wet, her cheeks red, as though she'd just been slapped across her face. What had I done? What had I said? I didn't even mean it! I'd just been so angry at Trisha for thinking she was better than me. How could I have said such stupid things?

"Philippa, I'm sorry, I—"

"Forget it, Daisy," she said coldly. Then without another word, she picked up her tray and got up. Lauren and Beth followed her.

I sat at the table on my own, staring into my bottle of water and wishing it could wash me away.

Daisy's words spun in my head, making me dizzy. I couldn't eat any more of my lunch. I would have been sick if I'd tried.

I'd gotten it all wrong. She was only being friendly to make her job easier. She didn't like me at all. Only moments earlier, I'd been thinking how well we were getting along — almost like best friends. What a fool.

I emptied the contents of my plate into the garbage and headed back to class on my own.

As I walked past the talent-show list, my legs nearly gave out. I wanted to scribble my name out or tear the list down. But a tiny voice somewhere, buried under everything else inside me was telling me that I had to do the talent show, even if I thought it would be the worst experience of my life. It was the only way I was ever going to get over the humiliation from years ago. If I could do this, I could do anything.

I had to trust that even though Daisy didn't really like me, at least she was serious about her job. She wanted to get it done and get back to Fairyland or wherever it was that she lived, so she'd make sure I got my wish.

I was sticking to my decision. I'd do the show.

Daisy and I didn't talk for the rest of the day. We didn't even meet each other's eyes. I couldn't bear to. I glanced at her briefly once or twice and thought she looked as miserable as I felt. She was probably thinking about how much more she would have enjoyed her assignment if she'd been Trisha Miles's fairy godsister instead. They'd have had *so* much fun. Well, tough! She was stuck with boring old me.

At home, I shut myself in my room for most of the evening. I just couldn't face talking to anyone. Mom was on the phone all evening anyway, and Dad was up in his study. He said not to disturb him.

The only thing that made me feel better was that I got a card from Charlotte. She must have sent it before she'd gotten my letter, so at least I didn't have to worry about her teasing me about fairies. I just couldn't have taken that at this point.

> Hi, Philippa!
>
> I got a pony! Her name is Magic. She's beautiful. It's all FABBBB here! Will catch up for real soon. Going riding in a minute! ☺
>
> How are you? Have you written yet? Tell me everything that's going on. I miss you sooooooooooooooooooooo much!
>
> Lots of love,
>
> Your best friend always, (I've still got the daisy chain. It's wilted a lot, but I pressed it in a book. I'm going to keep it always, like we said.)
>
> Charlotte xoxo

I had another pang of guilt as I realized I'd been so taken up with everything going on with Daisy that I'd hardly thought about Charlotte. Was I for-getting about her already—in less than a week? What kind of a best friend did that make me? No wonder Daisy didn't want to be my friend.

I sat in my room surrounded by my schoolbooks, trying to do my homework. I couldn't concentrate, though. I picked up a pack of cards and tried to practice a couple of tricks, but my heart wasn't even in that. I picked up more petals that had fallen onto the floor and straightened the daisy in its eggcup. Then I tried to think about anyone in the world whom I could talk to, or somewhere I could go where I wouldn't feel so alone. I came up blank. I didn't even have the tree house anymore. Even that was Daisy's now.

I decided to go to bed early. Maybe when I was asleep, I could at least dream of a more pleasant life than my real one.

I drifted off quickly, falling into a jittery, light sleep, just below the surface of wakeful awareness.

There was a tapping sound. I was in the woods, surrounded by tall trees, sunlight spiking down between them in pointy rays. A woodpecker. I stood and watched it tapping its head against the side of the tree. *Tap-tap-tap-tap-tap.* It stopped for a moment, turning its head to look at me. The tree turned to glass, and the woodpecker went back at it. *TAP-TAP-TAP-TAP.* Louder and faster.

Then — "Philippa!" Someone was calling me through the trees.

"Philippa!" *TAP! TAP! TAP!*

I opened my eyes.

I was in my bedroom, not the woods. There was no woodpecker; I was wide awake. But the tapping was still going on. What was it?

I got out of bed and crept over to the window. *Tap-tap-tap-tap-tap.* It was at my window! But that was impossible. My bedroom was upstairs! How could someone reach my window? A window cleaner? That was the best my sleepy brain could come up with. I glanced at my clock. It was nearly midnight. Not the window cleaner, then.

"Philippa!" The voice called again from outside. I realized who it was. I pulled the curtain back. And there she was, right outside my window. Daisy!

I just gaped at her. I didn't know what to say or how to make my voice say anything at all. Even though I knew what Daisy was, even though I'd even seen her wings, I still hadn't been prepared for this — a real, live fairy hovering outside my window, flying in the air in the middle of the night.

It was like something directly out of a book or a movie. Not out of real life — certainly not *my* life!

Her yellowy blond hair looked almost gold in the night sky; her school uniform had been replaced by what looked like white silk and feathers. Everything about her sparkled and shone, lighting up the space all around her. Her beautiful wings vibrated softly as she hovered in the air, right there in the dark night sky, their feathery tips flashing like sparklers as the moonlight hit them.

"Philippa, you have to come with me," Daisy said. "The next shooting star is in half an hour. You can make another wish."

I was about to leap into action and do exactly what she said. She *did* care about me after all. She wanted me to get my wish!

Then I remembered. She only wanted me to have my wishes as soon as possible so she could get her assignment done and get away from me. I had to remember that. It wasn't because she liked me; it wasn't because she wanted me to be happy. It was just a job, and she wanted it done. I must not ever forget that again.

Still, after the day I'd had, I knew instantly what I was going to wish for.

"I'll meet you in five minutes," I said. Then I pulled my robe on and, for the third time in a week, crept as silently as I could through the sleeping, silent house and out into the backyard.

Daisy was waiting for me inside the tree house.

"We've got about twenty minutes," she said, fumbling with the box that held the vouchers. "Do you know what you're going to wish for?"

"Yes," I said quietly.

Daisy looked up. It was the first time she'd met my eyes since lunchtime. I looked away.

"Look, Philippa, about before . . ."

"It doesn't matter," I said. "I know you're just here to do your job. You've told me enough times. It's not your fault that I thought for a moment there was anything more to it than that, or that I thought we were almost becoming friends."

"We *were* becoming friends. We *are* becoming friends."

"It didn't sound like it earlier."

Daisy dropped her head. "I know. I'm so sorry.

I can't believe I said those things. I didn't mean them. I just got so angry at Trisha in the heat of the moment. I don't seem to be able to think before I speak sometimes."

"Well, maybe the heat of the moment is when the truth comes out. If you didn't have time to stop and think about what you were saying, perhaps that means you spoke the truth."

"No, it's not like that, honestly. I—"

"Forget it, Daisy," I snapped. I wanted to believe her, but I'd been taken in once and I wasn't about to let her make a fool of me again. "I know where you stand, and it's fine. Just tell me where the star is coming from and what to do, and we'll be two-thirds of the way through your assignment. Then we've just got the final wish, and you're out of here."

Daisy fell silent. I looked over at her. Her face was gray. She looked smaller somehow. Her skin was pale in the moonlight, her face even thinner than usual. "That's what you want, isn't it?" I asked.

She let out a sigh. "No, it's, well, yes, I mean— look, I don't know what I want anymore. This assignment isn't what I was expecting."

"Don't worry about it. You don't need to say anything to make me feel better. In fact, it's best if you don't even try. You'll probably just make things worse. Let's just move on to what we're here to do."

Daisy nodded glumly. Then she handed me the envelope. "It's coming from the west; that's over there." She pointed to the window facing the house. "You'll probably see it come directly over the roof of your house."

"What time?"

Daisy checked her MagiCell. "12:35."

"OK. Five minutes, then."

I took the envelope to the window and opened it up. Colors sparkled and leaked all around my hands, flowing over me like warm water.

I could hear Daisy shuffling around behind me. She didn't say anything else to me, though. I didn't say anything to her, either. There was nothing more to say. We both knew exactly where we stood now, so we just had to deal with it.

"This is it. Ready?" Daisy held her MagiCell out in front of her, studying the screen. "Ten seconds."

I counted down in my head. Then, just as I'd

done last time, I held my arm right out the window into the night sky, the voucher in my open palm. Then I spoke out loud, as clearly as I could. My second wish was simple.

"I wish I were the most popular girl in school," I said.

Whoosh! The star came out of nowhere, zooming up from behind the house and over the roof, just as Daisy had said it would. It swept across the sky, zipping over the tree house, right over our heads, and whisking my wish away with it.

It was over in seconds.

Which left Daisy and me alone in the tree house again. And the blackness of the sky outside, surrounding us, made the silence between us even deeper.

"I'll just go back to the house," I said awkwardly.

Daisy was working on her MagiCell, punching buttons and frowning at the screen as she scribbled in one of the notebooks she seemed to have decided was hers now.

She looked up at me. "I'm going to make this one work really well," she said.

"I know you will," I replied, my voice coming

out a little harder than I intended. "It's your job, and you want to do it as well as you can."

Daisy sighed. "It's not just because it's my job, Philippa," she said. "I want to show you that I —"

"Save it, Daisy," I said firmly. "You don't need to tell me things just to make me feel better. I know how you feel. It'll be over soon."

She didn't say anything else. As we looked at each other, I almost thought I saw her eyes start to water. It was just the moonlight reflected in them, though. It must have been.

I climbed down the stairs. "See you in the morning," I said. Daisy just swallowed and nodded in reply.

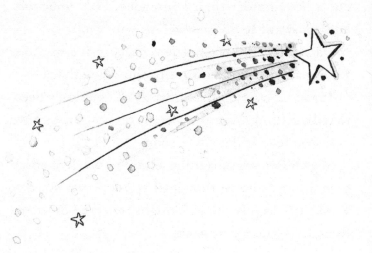

What was happening to me? Was I sick?

Fairy godmothers don't get sick! But I couldn't remember feeling like this before. It was a kind of pain in my throat. Not a pain exactly, just a feeling. Like something was stuck in there. Had I eaten something I shouldn't have? All I'd had all day were dandelion leaves and straw sticks. Had I drunk enough water?

But there was something else. My chest was tight. My eyes hurt. And what was that?

A drop of water fell onto my MagiCell. I looked up at the roof to see if there was a leak. It wasn't even raining.

My cheek was damp. What was happening to me?

I put down my MagiCell and my pen and leaned back against the tree-house wall. *Face it, Daisy. It's tears. You're crying. You're upset.*

But I didn't get upset! Certainly not over a human! I was too tough for that. Feelings like that were for wimps. I didn't *do* upset—ever since my friend was swatted dead. That was the last time I'd felt anything like this. In fact, ever since then, I'd hardly really done emotion at all, now that I thought about it.

Was that the problem? It wasn't only that I didn't get hurt; it was that I didn't really care at all. About anything. I never seemed to feel happy or have fun or laugh or smile or anything.

And what was the point of that?

I thought about Philippa doing her magic tricks and how nice it had felt to see her face shining with pleasure when I told her how good she was at it. I didn't really know much about that kind of feeling, to be honest. The kind that fills you up with much more pleasure than you can ever get if you go around not caring about people.

Suddenly, I *wanted* to feel; I wanted to care—even if it hurt sometimes. And I wanted Philippa to know I cared. Maybe it was too late, after what I'd done in the cafeteria. I could hardly believe I'd been so stupid and so horrible. I couldn't bear to think about it.

Maybe Philippa would never want to be my friend now, but at least I could try. All I wanted was to see her smile a little more.

Well, by the time I got her second wish in place, she'd definitely be doing that. And with a bit of luck, she'd remember who'd made it happen and maybe even forgive me. Perhaps we could even be friends.

One thing at a time. I had to get to work. I scribbled away in the notebook, writing down all the things I needed to organize before Monday.

The sun was starting to rise when I finally finished my report for ATC. I snuggled down as best I could on the blanket and fell into a smiling sleep.

chapter eleven
MISS POPULAR

Nothing worthy of note happened over the weekend. I spent most of it in my bedroom doing my homework and learning new magic tricks. I didn't go down to the tree house — I didn't want to see Daisy again. I didn't even reply to Charlotte's letter. I couldn't bring myself to write to her while I was feeling so low. She was enjoying her new life so much that it didn't feel fair to bring her down. I kept out of Mom and Dad's way, too, as far as I could. They seemed to spend half the weekend arguing and the other half ignoring each other. Welcome to the house of fun.

I heard them when I woke up on Monday morning. I couldn't tell what they were saying at first; I could just hear my mom's raised voice. My parents had never argued before, so at first I thought the TV was on really loud. But I crept to my bedroom door and opened it just enough to listen, and that's when I heard what they were saying.

"And whose perfume was it that you were wearing last night?" Mom was yelling.

"Perfume? I don't wear perfume!" Dad replied.

"Exactly! So who does? I bet it's that new girl in the office. She's been after you ever since she started there."

"Don't be ridiculous!"

"Ridiculous? *I'm* ridiculous?" Mom yelled back, her voice growing more and more high-pitched with each word. "I'm not the one acting like a teenage boy, staying out all hours and coming home stinking of whiskey and another woman's perfume!"

"I was *not* with Ann," Dad said firmly. "But I'll tell you something — it'll be a relief to get to work and see her. At least she gives me a smile in the morning. At least she can laugh without scheduling it in her planner!"

There was silence after that. I crept back into

my bedroom, closing the door as quietly as I could behind me. My hands shook as I got dressed.

By the time I came downstairs, they were both trying to act as though nothing had happened. Dad sat at the table with his paper as usual. Mom had my breakfast on the table for me, just like every day this week. I couldn't eat it, though.

"Are you ready?" Dad asked coldly as I picked at my egg.

I got up quickly. "Yep." I took my breakfast to the sink. "Sorry, Mom, I'm not very hungry this morning."

Mom gave me a tight, false smile. "Not to worry, darling. Make sure you have a good lunch."

"OK."

She stood in front of me awkwardly. She looked as though she wanted to say something else.

"What?" I asked.

Mom shook her head. "Nothing, dear. Have a good day."

"You too," I said. Then I reached out to give her a hug. She jumped a little, as though she'd gotten an electric shock. I put my arms around her, and she gave me a clumsy, halfhearted hug back. She couldn't even hug me properly.

"Off you go, dear," she said, letting me go as quickly as she could.

Dad had the radio on by the time I got in the car, and we didn't talk all the way to school. It was excruciating. I kept trying to think of ways to make conversation with him, but my mouth and my words dried up every time I tried. He didn't seem bothered. He didn't even look at me, just stared ahead and listened to his precious financial news.

By the time I got to school, I'd almost forgotten about Friday night's wish, so it took a moment to realize what was happening. It started the second I got out of the car.

"Hi, Phil."

"Hey, Phil."

"Morning, Phil. Want a hand with your books?"

I was almost dizzy by the time I got to the school door. I had to turn around to say hello to someone every other second. It seemed like the whole school knew me. I'd always been one of the ones no one noticed. I suppose I'd usually been fine with it that way. If they didn't notice you, at least nothing bad would happen. Secretly, though, I'd always wanted to be one of the ones who *was* noticed — but in a good way. And now, thanks to my wish, it was really happening! Everywhere I looked, people were smiling at me, waving at me, coming over to say hi. I felt like a movie star.

By the time Miss Holdsworth came into class to take attendance, I'd forgotten about my parents. Home life could wait. School was what I cared about right now. And boy, was I going to have a good day at school!

Daisy burst through the door just in time to hear her name called out. "Yes, Miss Holdsworth," she answered breathlessly. I turned away. I wasn't going to let Daisy bother me today. I didn't need her now, anyway. I could be friends with anyone I wanted.

She tried to catch my eye as she sat down, and I felt a bit bad for ignoring her. I mean, it *was* thanks to her that I *was* suddenly Miss Popular.

I turned to face her. "Thank you for the wish," I said as politely as I could. "I'm very grateful."

Daisy smiled such a big smile at me that for a moment I wanted to smile back and forgive her for what she'd done. I wanted to confide in her about Mom and Dad and laugh with her about how good it felt having everyone want to know me. I wanted to share all sorts of things with her — kind of like what you'd do with a best friend.

But I didn't. I had to remind myself that she didn't care about me. She didn't even like me. She was just doing her job. I was an assignment to her and nothing more. I could not forget that again.

So I turned away from her and opened my geography book.

Five minutes into the lesson, Lauren passed a note across the table to me while Miss Holdsworth was writing something on the board. I grabbed the note and opened it below my desk.

Me and Beth aren't going to be best friends anymore. We both want to be yours! Have you decided which of us you want to be best friends with?

I looked up at Lauren. She was smiling hopefully at me. Lauren and Beth both wanted to be my best friend? But they'd been best friends for ever! They were like two halves of an orange. I couldn't imagine them not being best friends.

I scribbled a note and shoved it back across to Lauren.

Let's all be best friends!

For a second, she looked disappointed. But a moment later, she glanced up at me and nodded. "OK," she mouthed.

That was one thing taken care of, then. I didn't have to worry about hanging around on my own anymore. I mean, Lauren and Beth had tried to include me since Charlotte had left, but I could tell their hearts hadn't really been in it. Now I knew they really wanted to hang around with me. I didn't need to feel like the third wheel. And I *certainly* didn't need Daisy!

I looked around the class, my mind wandering as Miss Holdsworth talked about contours and map coordinates. As I scanned the room, it seemed that everyone I looked at turned and smiled at me. I could probably be best friends with anyone I wanted! Maybe I didn't even have to settle for Lauren and Beth. Not that there was anything wrong with them, really. But we'd never been the most popular foursome in the class. We'd never been the group that everyone admired and revered. That was reserved for Trisha's gang.

That was when I realized — perhaps even Trisha

Miles would want to be my friend. Was fairy magic that powerful? A second later, Trisha turned and gave me a wink. "Meet me at break," she whispered.

It was! It really was powerful enough to turn sworn enemies into friends! Trisha Miles wanted me to meet up with her during our break! Lauren and Beth could wait.

Trisha was waiting for me at the other end of the playground. Her end of the playground. I hesitated for a moment. Maybe it was a trick. I just couldn't honestly believe that Trisha Miles really wanted to spend time with me.

Come on, there's only one way to find out. I dragged my shaky legs across the playground toward her, stopping every few seconds to say hi to someone.

"Have a good trip?" Trisha asked with a laugh as a fifth-grade girl, smiling at me as she walked past us, stumbled on a loose paving stone. "Send us a postcard next time!"

Trisha nudged me, and I forced myself to laugh. I knew by now that when Trisha Miles makes a joke, you laugh. Either that or you end up being the subject of her next joke — which will be even less funny than the one before it.

I tried to think of something witty to say back to her. That's when it occurred to me that Trisha's jokes always seemed to be at the expense of someone else, and I couldn't bring myself to make fun of anyone else. Not when I knew what it felt like to be on the receiving end of jokes like that. And especially not when everyone was being so nice to me!

I didn't have to worry for long. Within two minutes, there was a crowd around us. Well, around me.

"Hey, Phil, I like your hair today. Have you done something different with it?"

"Phil, where did you get your shoes? I'm going to ask my mom if I can get some just like yours."

"Hey, Phil, want some candy? I've got caramel chews and vanilla fudge. They're my favorites, but you can have whichever you like."

"Hey, Phil, which side of the bed did you get up on this morning? I'm going to get up on the same side of mine tomorrow."

OK, so I made the last one up. But it could almost have been true. I didn't even have time to answer most of what was said to me, because someone else was busy asking me another question. In the end, all I could do was laugh—and eat a handful of caramel chews.

This was the best day of my life!

"Come on, Phil, let's get away from these guys." Trisha pulled on my sleeve.

"But I—" I wanted to say I was enjoying myself. I knew better than to argue with Trisha, though. And that was another thing. She'd called me Phil, just like all the others. I'd *always* wanted to be called Phil. Phil sounded like someone cool and popular—two things I've never been, so I'd never told anyone that was what I wanted to be called. I didn't want to run the risk of being laughed at and told I could never be a Phil. I'd always be boring old Philippa.

Not anymore! I *was* cool and popular now, so Phil suited me just fine — even if it did still sound a little bit strange hearing it out loud.

I wandered off with Trisha. "Hey, I'm getting sick of being followed by a mob all the time," she complained. "Aren't you?"

"Um . . ."

"I mean, they just won't leave us alone. We're like the most popular girls in the school, aren't we?"

I wanted to say that actually it was just me who was the most popular girl in the school. "Yeah, we are," I said instead.

I kind of ran out of things to say after that. I didn't want to put my foot in my mouth and risk saying anything that would make her turn on me. I didn't want to try and say something funny and have her not laugh. I didn't want to try and say anything too clever in case it sounded boring or as if I were trying to show off. I felt trapped.

"How about I come over to your house after school?" Trisha said.

"Really?" I breathed. Trisha wanted to see me outside of school! She wanted to hang out with *me*!

"Sure, I'll ask my mom when she comes to pick me up."

"Great!" I said with a grin. Two seconds later, we were mobbed again. As we headed back into school at the end of break, in between saying hi to about twenty more people, I tried to make a mental list of things that Trisha and I could talk about later. I didn't want to risk any more of those awkward silences.

"So what should we do?" Trisha was standing in the kitchen looking bored while I fixed us some lemonade.

"Um, we could just, um, hang out? Read some magazines or . . ." My voice trailed away. Charlotte and I used to make up stories together. I didn't dare suggest anything like that. Trisha would probably make me a laughingstock at school if I did.

"Haven't you got a PlayStation or anything?"

I laughed. Mom hated computer games almost as much as she hated industrial farming. The old mom did, anyway. Perhaps New Mom would buy me a PlayStation! I wouldn't ask her today, though. She looked even more miserable than she had this morning. She hadn't even bothered to try and smile when she picked me up. I think she was glad I asked if Trisha could come over, so she wouldn't have to worry about me hanging around her once we got home.

"Not yet," I said. "I might get one for Christmas, though."

Trisha rolled her eyes. "Hey, what's that down there?" she asked, looking out into the yard. I went over to see what she was looking at.

"What's what?"

She pointed down to the bottom of the backyard. "That thing in the middle of the trees."

"That's my tree house!" I said excitedly.

"Cool. Let's see it."

As we made our way down the yard, it occurred to me that Daisy might be in there. We hadn't really talked at school, other than the occasional comment in class. I'd hardly had the chance anyway, with all the others crowding around me.

By the end of the day, I'd felt really mean. At lunchtime, she sat eating her strange salad and drinking bottlefuls of water on her own. She was at a table with some others, but I could tell she wasn't really part of the group. She was just sitting there looking down at her food, her head drooping, avoiding meeting people's eyes, and acting as though she didn't really mind that no one was talking to her.

Part of me wanted to run over and sit by her. I wanted to tell her how crazy it was having everyone in the school wanting to talk to me and be my friend, and how my cheekbones were starting to hurt from the amount of smiling back that I was doing. I wanted to just laugh with her — I guess I felt that I could talk to her about anything. I don't know why I felt that; I just did.

Then I remembered not to fall into that trap again. I wasn't going to let her — or anyone — make a fool out of me.

"Let's sit over there," Trisha had said, pointing to a table over at the other side of the cafeteria. I didn't look at Daisy as we passed.

Thinking about it now, I really did wish I'd gone over to sit with her instead. Maybe I could have been hanging out with her in the tree house now, instead of with Trisha. I never wondered what to talk about when I was with Daisy.

Maybe I'd misjudged her. I mean, sure, I knew I was just a job to her. But she didn't really *have* to be nice to me, did she? I mean, she *had* apologized for being mean in the cafeteria, and I'd realized today how much we all wanted to be in with the in-crowd. I wanted it. I always had. I couldn't blame Daisy for wanting the same thing.

As we approached the tree house, I found myself hoping that Daisy would be there so I could apologize—again. If she wanted to be friends with me, then I wanted it, too. She'd made two wishes come true for me now, and she'd been trying her hardest to be nice to me all day, and I'd just ignored her. I wanted to make things right as soon as possible.

But I was *really* hoping more for the opposite—that actually Daisy would be nowhere *near* the tree house. Trisha would be in there with me, and I couldn't run the risk of her finding out about Daisy.

"So, it was good hanging out at school today, wasn't it?" I said really loudly as we approached the tree house. "And now we're going to hang out in my TREE HOUSE."

Trisha gave me a strange look. "Are you all right?" she asked.

"I'm FINE!" I shouted. "I'm just really excited about showing you the TREE HOUSE."

She nodded slowly and carefully. "OK," she said nervously.

Then I had a thought. "Let me just show you the woods around the back first." If Daisy had heard me, which she must have if she was up there, it would give her a chance to get away.

"What d'you think?" I asked, perching on the fence that separated our yard from the woods.

"What do I think about what?" Trisha replied.

"The woods. They're good, aren't they?"

She raised an eyebrow. "I guess they're OK, if you like that kind of thing. I'd rather have the Tamdale Center."

The Tamdale Center is the big mall in town, full of stores and fast food and arcades. I already knew that Trisha liked to spend every Saturday there. I'd seen her a couple of times when I was doing some shopping with Mom.

"Come on, I'll show you the tree house," I said, skimming through my mental lists in search of something—anything—that we might have in common to talk about.

Trisha shuddered as she looked at the ladder. "Do I have to climb up that?"

"It's the only way to get in there," I said with a grin.

"You first."

I scooted up to the trapdoor and had a quick look around. Empty, thank goodness.

"Come on up," I called down to Trisha.

"I'm coming. Give me a chance." She fumbled her way up the ladder and dragged herself into the tree house.

"This is it," I said, holding my arms out wide.

"OK." She didn't look impressed.

"This is my favorite place in the whole world."

She raised that eyebrow again. "Really? Why?"

"Don't you think it's amazing? A little house all my own in the middle of the trees, where you can do anything you like and be separate from the rest of the world."

"Anything you like? You can't go shopping."

"No, of course you can't do that, but —"

"Or play a video game."

"I don't want to do those things!" I said.

"So what *do* you do in here?" Trisha asked, looking around disdainfully.

"Well, I — I read, I do puzzles, I make up stories..." My voice faltered and trailed off. I sounded so lame. And I certainly wasn't going to tell her about the magic!

"Sounds like a blast," she said sarcastically. She

wandered around the tree house, searching for anything that might hold any interest for her—and clearly failing, if her exaggerated sighs of boredom were anything to go by. I was starting to wonder why I'd ever thought hanging out with Trisha Miles would be such a wonderful thing to do.

All those years I'd looked at her and her friends, wishing they would like me, wishing I could be part of their gang, thinking how great my life would be if I were in their group, how it would show the world that I'd arrived and I was worth something. And now that I'd actually made it, now that Trisha saw me as someone worth hanging out with, I discovered it wasn't that exciting at all. In fact, Trisha Miles was *boring*! The only reason that everyone wanted to be in her gang was so they wouldn't be on the receiving end of her meanness. It was crystal clear now.

I tried to think of a way to get out of hanging out with her. I could say I had tons of homework to do, but she'd probably only make fun of me if I said that—even if I *was* the most popular girl in the school! I could say I was feeling ill or tired, but then she might just think I was even more of a wimp than she already thought I was. I was still desperately trying to think of something when I noticed her eyes fall on the box with the final wish voucher in it.

"What's this?" she asked, picking it up.

"That? Oh, it's nothing, just an old box," I said quickly. "I haven't picked it up for ages. There's probably not even anything in it." I held my hand out for the box. "Here, let me have a look," I said as casually and calmly as I could.

But Trisha ignored me. She was busy opening it.

"Hey, I think there's something really good on TV in a minute," I said, trying desperately to distract her. "Shall we go and see?"

"Sure, in a sec," Trisha said. "Hey, what's this?" She had the envelope in her hand.

"Oh, it's nothing, probably just an old bill of Dad's, or something," I said with a laugh that even I could tell was about as false as a wax model. *Don't open it, don't open it!*

Trisha looked inside the envelope. "There's something in here. Wow, it's really colorful. It's like there's a light on inside it!"

"Ah, no, I know what that is," I said, my mind completely blank. *Think of something, think of something. Make her put it down!*

KERRASHH!

Trisha and I both leaped about a foot in the air. What was *that*?

We ran over to the window to see what it had been. At first we couldn't see anything. Then I noticed it. A huge branch had fallen off one of the old trees, crashing down on one of the other trees. How had that happened?

Mom was on her way out of the house.

"Come on," I said. "Let's go and see what's happened."

Thankfully, Trisha had dropped the envelope and forgotten about it now. She followed me down the ladder.

"What's happened? What have you girls been up to? Are you all right?" Mom asked. I tried not to notice that my well-being was only third on the list.

"We're fine, Mom," I said. "Look, it's one of the oldest trees; it must have just fallen over. Maybe the woodpeckers got to it."

"Yes, well, I'll get your father to have a look at it later," she said, walking around the tree and examining it. "If he has the *time*, that is," she added scornfully. She started walking back to the house.

"As long as you're all right," she said as an after-thought.

"We're fine, Mom. We're coming back in now."

I started following Mom up to the house.

"I forgot my bag," Trisha said. "Hang on."

She scuttled back to the tree house. Half a minute later she returned. "Not there," she said. "I must have left it in the house."

As we walked up to the house, I wondered how much more dire the afternoon could get, and if there was anything I could think of to make Trisha want to leave sooner.

"Oh, no, I just remembered something," she said, slapping her forehead as we reached the house. "I said I'd help my dad with something this evening. I completely forgot." She looked at her watch. "He'll be home any minute. You know, I think I should go."

"Really?" I said, trying not to sound too hopeful. "You're sure you have to leave?"

Trisha looked as though she were considering it.

No! Don't change your mind! Go!

"I think I should," she said. "I don't want to let him down. You know what parents are like, making you feel guilty when you don't do things you said you would."

Actually, I didn't know what it was like at all. My previous parents — whom I missed more and more with every passing moment — never gave me a hard time about anything. They just let me be who I was and were totally proud of me, whatever I did. And if I ever let them down over anything, they always said they understood. My current parents didn't seem to notice what I did either way.

"Yeah, I know what you mean," I said.

We'd stopped in the hallway. "Oh, there it is. Silly me," Trisha said, picking up her bag. "Well, look, this has been fun. Let's do it again soon."

"Of course!" I said with a great big false smile that matched hers.

"OK, cool. Well, see you at school tomorrow," she said, opening the front door.

"Yeah, see you," I said. I stood and waved while she headed off down the street. The moment she was out of sight, I went back inside, closed the door behind me, and fell back against it with utter relief. Thank goodness that was over. Trisha obviously felt the same way. She'd been as desperate to get away as I had.

That was close!

Another second and she'd have pulled the wish voucher out and seen everything. In the wrong hands, those vouchers can be lethal. You don't know what a girl like Trisha might do with one. And if she held on to it without making a wish before the end of my life cycle—well, it didn't bear thinking about. If I didn't wrap up the assignment and get out of here in a couple of days, I'd never live to get another assignment.

No, I wasn't going to think about that. Anyway—well, it just wouldn't happen. It couldn't.

I refused to think about it anymore. I couldn't let myself. I'd never finish the job if I let those worries take hold of me.

I know it was a bit drastic, making the tree collapse like that, but I had to think quickly, and it was the best I could come up with. At least it did the trick.

It was just as well that Philippa gave me so much warning on the way there, too. Quick thinking on her part. I really had underestimated her. But I'd already figured that much out. The bit I hadn't worked out yet was how to make her give *me* another chance.

It had been really uncomfortable, scrunching up in the trunk of a tree like that, but at least I'd kept myself out of sight. I hated it. Not just because it was a tight squeeze in the tree. Not because of that at all, actually.

I hated that she was in the tree house with Trisha. I know it's stupid, but I kind of thought of the tree house as our place now. I didn't want her in there with someone else. I don't know why she'd want to be friends with Trisha, anyway. I know I'd thought Trisha was my kind of person at first, but she wasn't. She wasn't the kind of person I'd want to *be*, anyway.

I'd rather be like Philippa.

OK, so Philippa wasn't the coolest girl in the school. Even *with* the popularity wish! And maybe her hair was a little crazy and her friends were sort of geeky—but she was funny, and clever, and kind. And I was determined to show her that I could be those things, too.

My head was full of all these thoughts as I flew back into the tree house.

I started cleaning up, and that's when I saw it. The box. It was open. And empty.

No! Where was the envelope? Where *was* it?

I searched all around, trying to stem the rising panic I could feel from my toes to the tips of my wings. The envelope *had* to be here somewhere.

But it wasn't. I searched the whole tree house from top to bottom, three times over. That was it. Definitely.

The final wish was gone.

chapter twelve
THE MISSING WISH

It was only after Trisha left that I noticed the envelope in the hall addressed to me. I tore it open.

> *Dear Philippa,*
>
> *Thank you! It was so great to hear from you. You really made me laugh. Even now, when we're hundreds of miles apart, you still manage to think of ways to make me laugh. I love it that you remembered us talking about fairies and how much it entertained me. You should go onstage as a comedian!*

I couldn't read any more. She hadn't believed me about Daisy. I knew she wouldn't. Would I have believed her if it was the other way around? I didn't know. Suddenly I felt as if Charlotte and I didn't know each other at all. And telling me to go onstage just reminded me that I hadn't even shared the news about the talent show with her either. We used to share everything. Now she almost felt like a stranger. How had it happened so quickly?

I couldn't answer any of the questions filling my mind. I just knew I had something more important to do.

I was halfway down the yard when I heard something hissing at me.

"*Psst. Pssst!*"

I looked around. What was it? Where was it coming from? It sounded like a snake!

"Philippa! It's me, Daisy!"

I looked across to the tree house. The top of her head was poking out of the window as she peeked around to check that no one else had seen her.

"I'm on my way!" I scrambled up the ladder. "Oh, Daisy, I'm so glad to see you!" I said, my words falling out of me in a rush. "I've been really unfair to you. You said you were sorry for what you did the other day, and I was so mean about it. I know you meant well, and I do really want us to be friends and to get —"

"There's no time for that now!"

"Oh." I felt as though she'd pulled out a plug and deflated me. "I thought you might want us to be friends. I guess I got it wrong — again." I turned back to the ladder.

Daisy grabbed my arm. "No!"

"I'm sorry I troubled you. I won't do it again."

"No! You're wrong! I mean, you're right!"

I stared at her. "Which?"

"I *do* want us to be friends. I really, really do!"

"You do?" I turned back to her. She was smiling. At least, her mouth was turned upward as though she wanted me to think she was smiling. Her eyes were doing something completely different though. They looked pinched and tense.

"I honestly do," she said again. "But something terrible has happened."

"What is it?"

Daisy picked up the box with the last wish voucher in it. As soon as she held it out toward me, I knew. Even before I opened it. "She took it," I said, looking inside the empty box. But how? She'd dropped the box when that branch fell off the tree.

"It must have been when she went back to get her bag," Daisy said, reading my thoughts, like a best friend would.

How could I have been so stupid? Of *course* she had taken the voucher. That was *exactly* the kind of thing Trisha Miles would do. And that was why she'd been so eager to get away. Why had I thought it would be so great to have her as my friend? In all these years of wanting to be in her gang, there was one minor detail I'd forgotten. I didn't actually like her! And I never had.

"What are we going to do?" I asked.

Daisy chewed on a finger as she started to pace the tree house. "I don't know yet," she said. "I've already checked the MagiCell and there aren't any shooting stars tonight. There's just the one on Tuesday."

Tuesday. The one I needed if I was going to get through Wednesday's talent show in one piece.

"But she wouldn't know what to do anyway, would she?"

"They've got instructions on the back, about doing it at the time of the shooting stars and all that," Daisy said glumly. "They're scrambled up in code, but she might be able to pick her way through it."

I remembered the line of strange symbols across the back of the vouchers, and my spirits lifted a bit. "Trisha Miles couldn't crack a code if she had the answer book in front of her! She doesn't do things like that. We'll be fine," I said. "Anyway, the chances of her making a wish at exactly the right time must be slim," I added hopefully.

Daisy nodded. There was something else, though, I could tell.

"What?" I asked.

She shook her head. "Nothing. It's fine." She tried to smile, but behind the smile, I noticed with a shock how frail she was starting to look. Her face was thin and drawn; her eyes had dark patches below them; her hair was limp and thin. It was even starting to fall out. Just like the petals of the daisy in my bedroom.

"What is it?" I insisted.

"It's just — I've only got a couple of days," she said.

"Then what happens?"

"If you haven't made your three wishes, the

assignment won't be completed in time. I simply have to get the wish back to you."

"And what if you don't?" I asked, my words fighting to get around the stone in my throat. I knew the answer. I just wanted her to tell me I was wrong. She didn't.

Daisy looked straight at me. For a moment, I thought I saw fear in her eyes—but I must have been wrong. I couldn't imagine Daisy being afraid of anything. I thought again of the daisy in my bedroom. It would die soon; I knew that.

"That just isn't an option," she said eventually. Then she got out her MagiCell, and I knew the subject was closed. It was better that way.

But as she punched buttons and jotted down notes, I felt the determination growing inside me, rising up like a volcano, building up and growing and bubbling away. "Daisy," I said calmly, "we'll get it back."

She looked up and gave me a brief smile. "Let's just get to work," she said.

Tuesday started the same way as the day before. I was practically mobbed from the moment I got out of the car.

In class, even Miss Holdsworth seemed to be acting differently toward me. "Now, let's have everyone sitting up straight, nice and neat and quiet, and showing me you're ready, just like Philippa," she said, smiling at me.

Everyone turned to stare at me. I could feel my cheeks burn up, but it wasn't like it had been in the past. I didn't want to disappear on the spot. I still felt embarrassed by the attention, but it was nice attention. As I waited for my cheeks to stop burning, I realized that being the center of attention didn't have to be all that bad. For the first time ever, it crossed my mind that perhaps I could get over what had happened all those years ago — and maybe even put it behind me one day.

Every pair of eyes that looked at me had admiration in them. As the rest of the class turned back to face the teacher, half of them had folded their arms in exactly the same way as me.

In fact, while I was looking around at the class, I noticed something else. At least five of the girls had changed their hairstyles. They all used to have long, silky straight hair, but they'd clearly been messing with mousse and cream so their hair had fuzzed up and was sticking out at all sorts of angles. Just like mine! I'd spent years wishing that my hair would behave and look straight and normal like everyone else's, and now they'd all gone out and spent money on products to make their hair look like mine!

At morning break, Daisy pulled me over to one corner of the playground.

"Have you got a plan yet?" I asked, looking around to check that no one was listening.

"If we can find some way to distract her for long enough today, we can check her bag and desk. Maybe you can take her off somewhere with you, and I'll search her things while you're gone."

"OK—but what if I can't distract her for long enough?"

"Then you'll have to go over to her house tonight, and we'll do it there."

"Oh, no! I don't think I could stand another evening in her company!"

"It's the only thing I can think of," Daisy said.

"Well, we'll have to try our hardest to do it before school finishes."

"OK."

That was all we had time for before a band of fourth-grade girls crowded around, asking me questions and laughing at the slightest thing I said that could possibly pass as a joke. Daisy and I soon got separated.

At lunchtime, we were walking down the hallway together, trying to figure out a way to get Trisha away from her bag.

I was surrounded again as we went into the cafeteria.

"Phil, I've saved you a seat!"

"Phil, over here."

"Phil, do you want to sit with us?"

"Phil, you can share my chips, if you like."

My neck was aching from swiveling around to smile at everyone who spoke to me. I almost wanted to walk out. I mean, yes, I wanted to be popular. I wanted to be liked. I wanted to be in with the in-crowd. But something about all this attention was starting to feel weird, and kind of wrong.

The truth was, I wanted to be liked because of who I was, not because I'd made a wish. These people didn't really like me for myself. They just liked me because of some fairy magic that *made* them like me.

And there was something else. I was starting to get sick of being called Phil. It wasn't me. It was some fantasy of who I thought I could be. But whatever happened because of a wish, and whatever I might have thought I wanted, the truth was that I was no different from who I'd been before. If people couldn't like me for who I was before I made the wish, what was the point of making them think they liked me now?

For the first time since I'd made this wish, I began to think I'd made yet another mistake. Having three wishes just wasn't turning out to be all that easy to get right.

"There she is!" Daisy whispered, nudging me and nodding her head over to the opposite side of the cafeteria where Trisha was sitting with her gang. Even *they* waved and smiled when I looked in their direction. "You join them," Daisy said. "I'll head back to the classroom."

"But has Trisha got her bag with her?" I asked, craning my neck to see what was on the seat beside her.

"I can't see it. But even if she does, I'll look in her desk."

"OK, but be careful. Don't let Miss Holdsworth

catch you in the classroom. We're not allowed in there at all during lunch."

"I know. I'll be OK."

Then I had a thought. "Daisy, why can't you just use your MagiCell to get it back?"

Daisy shook her head. "I've tried that. The wish vouchers are more powerful than a single fairy's magic. If they're out of my possession, my MagiCell is no use in tracking them."

"But what about your boss? 3WD or whatever they're called? Can't they do something?"

"You're joking! They've nearly taken me off the case already! If they knew I'd messed up again, I'd be off this assignment before you could say, 'Sprinkle me with fairy dust and throw me to the bees.'"

I couldn't quite imagine why I'd be likely to say, "Sprinkle me with fairy dust and throw me to the bees," but I did get her point.

"Meet me at the playground in fifteen minutes," she said.

A minute later, she was gone, and I was heading over to Trisha's table with my sandwich and chips.

"Hey, Phil, sit next to me," Trisha said, shuffling along the bench. As she did, I noticed her bag by her side. Daisy would have to hope there was something in her desk. "Move over, Jacqui."

Jacqui looked slightly miffed to be demoted from her position next to Trisha. But when she realized it meant I'd be sitting next to her, too, she gave me a beaming smile. I stared at her. She'd never smiled at me — ever. I couldn't smile back. It was all starting to feel too fake. "Hey, Phil, you can have some of my chips if you like," she said.

"It's Philippa," I said quietly.

"What?" Trisha turned to me.

"I don't want to be called Phil anymore," I said, my hands clenched under the table. Was I really talking back to Trisha Miles? What did I think I was *doing*? I was going to be the laughingstock of the school all over again. "If that's OK with you," I added quickly.

"Cool," Trisha said. "Did you hear that, everyone? It's Philippa from now on, and anyone who calls her Phil will have me to answer to!"

I turned to see if she was being sarcastic. She gave me a wink and a nod. "Done," she said.

I stared down at my lunch. This was all getting too bizarre. When I looked up again, I noticed

Lauren and Beth sitting down at the next table. They both gave me a quick, shy wave. I was about to wave back when Trisha burst out laughing.

"Look at the geeks. They think they can be your friends—as if!" she said. "Go crack a code!" she called over to them. Then she nudged me, which I guessed was my cue to laugh along with her and say something mean about Lauren and Beth.

No, I couldn't. I wouldn't. I just wasn't going to do what Trisha wanted. I wasn't! I felt as though I were standing on a wobbly floor. Trisha had always made my insides quake with worry and doubt. But for once, instead of trying to scramble away to somewhere that didn't wobble, I stood still and firm and waited for the quaking to stop. I wasn't going to let her make me do *anything*.

After a while, she shrugged and got back to her lunch.

I'd done it! I wasn't exactly sure what had just happened, but I knew it was important.

"Hey, that's a thought!" Trisha said through a mouthful of chips. "I might have a quick word with them, after all. You don't mind, do you, Phil—I mean Philippa?"

"No, of course not. Go ahead," I replied as she

disappeared to Lauren and Beth's table — taking her bag with her.

I polished off my lunch, trying to join in the conversation around me — especially as it mostly seemed to center on me. My hair, my clothes, my shoes, the hilarious things I said in class, the brilliant story I'd written yesterday.

But as the conversation went on, I was more interested in what was going on at the next table. Trisha had taken something out of her bag. A piece of paper. She was giving it to Lauren and Beth and asking them something. They all looked really serious, studying the paper and nodding intently.

"End of the day," I heard her say as she got up and came back to join us.

What did she want them to do by the end of the day? Something told me it wasn't a good idea to ask. But Lauren and Beth? Trisha Miles didn't bother asking anything of them. Unless it was something she couldn't do herself. Like her science homework, or math tests or —

Oh, no!

No! She couldn't have!

"Just getting a bit of help with spelling for tomorrow's test," she said with a smile.

"Sorry, got to go," I said, edging out of my seat as Trisha sat back down. "Bathroom break." My voice must have been about as convincing as her lie about the spelling test. I didn't care. I had to get away and take care of this before it was too late. I had to get Lauren and Beth on their own. More importantly, I had to talk to Daisy.

I didn't hang around for a reply. Just gave a quick, apologetic look to Trisha and the others and made a speedy exit.

Once out of the cafeteria, I ran down the hallway, back to the classroom.

"Daisy!" I said, bursting through the door so hard it made her jump. She was standing by Trisha's desk, rummaging around inside the drawer, and slammed it shut as I came in the classroom.

"Nothing here," she said as I closed the door and joined her by Trisha's desk.

"I know. She must have it in her bag. She's got it with her."

"We'll have to think of —"

"Daisy!" I interrupted her. "She's been talking to Lauren and Beth."

"Really? I didn't think she liked them."

"Exactly! She gave them a piece of paper with something on it."

"What kind of piece of paper?" Daisy said slowly.

"I don't know for sure, but look — she knows they like cracking codes. She even made a joke about it in the cafeteria."

"You think she's given them the wish?"

I shook my head. "It was just an ordinary piece of paper, but I think she's written down the code from the back of it and asked them to unscramble it."

Daisy breathed out. "We'll have to stop them," she said.

"I know. And we've only got till the end of the day."

Daisy pulled out her bottle of water from her bag. "Philippa," she said after taking a huge glug. She sounded breathless. "I'm running out of energy." She sat down on Trisha's seat. She looked so frail. Her school uniform seemed to be hanging off her, as if it were four sizes too big.

I was about to reply when I heard the classroom door open. I spun around to see who it was.

Trisha Miles was standing in the doorway.

Trisha stepped into the classroom. "Looking for something?" she asked, sauntering over toward us.

"I just dropped something on the floor. Daisy was helping me. I —"

"Save it, Phil," Trisha said.

"It's Philippa," I said, trying to hold the confidence I'd had earlier. The wobble in my voice gave me away, though.

"Not to me, it isn't," Trisha said. "You see, I've worked out what's going on. I know why suddenly everyone wants to know you, why everyone talks about you constantly — 'Phil' this, 'Phil' that— why no one's quite so bothered about *me* anymore."

"I can't help it if they like me, can I?" I said nervously, hoping she couldn't see my fingernails digging into my palms by my sides.

"Can't you?" she sneered, taking a step closer to me. "Well, that was what I thought, too. I even thought I liked you myself, thought how lucky I was to have you hang out with me. Then I realized it was because of this!" With that, she reached into her bag and pulled something out. I hardly even had to look. I knew what it was going to be: the envelope with the final wish voucher.

"It's mine," I said weakly.

"Not anymore," Trisha said. "Finders keepers, losers weepers. And I think you'll find that *you're* the *loser!*"

"Give it back to her," Daisy said, pulling herself up from the chair.

"Yeah, that's another thing," Trisha said, rubbing her chin as she studied Daisy. "Where exactly do you fit into all this, new girl?"

"Daisy's got nothing to do with it," I said quickly.

Trisha shrugged. "Well, whatever. It doesn't matter to me. Won't matter to you either, by the end of today. Your nice little geeky friends will have told me everything I need to know by then."

"What will you do?" I asked.

"I haven't made my mind up yet. I might use the wish on something for myself. Or I might just rip it up so that no one can use it. Then again, I might use it to get you back for fooling me and the rest of the school into thinking you're popular."

"I didn't fool anyone," I said.

"Matter of opinion. Do you think anyone would look twice at you if you hadn't tricked them with a wish? Who would want to hang out with you?" Trisha laughed.

I didn't have an answer. She was right. Why *would* anyone want to hang out with me? Who was I trying to kid? Suddenly the whole thing felt ridiculous. My second wish hadn't improved my life at all. All it had done was make me realize how empty and false all these supposed new friendships were. Trisha was right. It was a trick. And not a very good one, either.

"*I* would," Daisy said from behind me.

"You would what?" Trisha asked.

"*I'd* look twice. I'd want to be friends with Philippa," she said. With a quick glance at me, she added, "She's worth a million of you, and if you do anything to hurt her, you'll have me to deal with as well."

Trisha studied us both. Then she burst out laughing. "Oooh, I'm so scared!" she said. "How will I be able to stand up to the pair of you!" She turned and headed back to the door, throwing her head back and laughing again.

"Have a nice day," she trilled, waving the envelope over her shoulder as she left us alone in the classroom.

Daisy and I stood in silence. I only had until tonight to think of a way around this. Just a few hours before Trisha would get her chance to destroy every bit of my life that wasn't already ruined.

I grabbed Lauren and Beth on their way back into class. "Hey," I said, sauntering in between them and linking arms with them both. "So, I thought we should talk about the idea of us all being best friends. What do you think?"

They both looked at me as though I'd just told them they'd each won a scholarship to the country's top science school.

"Definitely!" Beth grinned.

"Really?" Lauren breathed.

"Really! Of course. Who else would I want to be best friends with?"

"Well, we thought you might want to be Trisha's best friend," Beth said. "You've been hanging out with her lately."

"Trisha? Nah, she's not as much fun as you two." I paused for a moment before carrying on in the most casual voice I could squeeze out of my trembling mouth. "Hey, actually, she and I were playing a game earlier. We both had to crack a code, and I was thinking, seeing as we're all best friends now"—I flashed them another big smile and squeezed their linked arms even closer—"that you might be able to help me out."

"Of course we'll help you!" Lauren said excitedly.

"Great. Well, you see, as part of the game—and this would really help me to win, and I'd be so grateful and want to reward you as much as I could—I was thinking it would be really good fun if you could somehow give Trisha a false answer if she asked you to help her crack any codes or anything like that. Doesn't that sound like fun?"

I forced out a laugh that verged on hysterical. But neither of them laughed back. In fact, they stopped walking, and both looked at me with faces as heavy as the clouds that I could see starting to bunch up outside the window.

"We've already helped her," Lauren said, her voice utterly crestfallen and flat. "We just gave it to her now."

"We would never have done it if we'd known it was a game against you," Beth added.

"We probably got it wrong, anyway," Lauren added. "It didn't make any sense."

"Oh," I said, trying to sound light. "So, what was the answer that you gave her?" My voice rose a couple of octaves higher than usual. I was going to have to work on my casual-and-light voice if I was planning to get into any more of these situations. This couldn't really be convincing anyone.

Beth glanced at me. "It was just something like, 'Valid only at the time of a shooting star.' It didn't make any sense."

"I'm sure we got it wrong," said Lauren again.

I dropped their arms. "Yeah," I said. "You probably did."

"But we're still all best friends, aren't we?" she said hopefully.

"What? Oh, yes. Sure, whatever."

Beth took hold of my arm again and linked it through hers. "Great," she said, grinning as though no one's world had just collapsed.

I wiggled out of her grip. "Look, I'll catch up with you," I said. "I've just got to do something."

I waited until they'd gone into class, then I turned and headed for the bathroom. Locking myself into a stall, I put the lid down and sat, trying to figure out what we could do. No matter how I looked at it, the situation was completely hopeless. I'd lost my last wish, so I couldn't wish for confidence at the talent show. I was going to have to stand up in front of the entire school without it. It was pretty much my biggest nightmare. Not only that, but if Trisha somehow found out when the next shooting star was, she'd know exactly when she had to make her wish.

And whatever she wished for, one thing could be guaranteed: She wasn't going to be aiming to make *my* life any better. And I couldn't even begin to think about what would happen to Daisy if she failed at this assignment.

I sat in my bedroom, my schoolbooks all around me. I couldn't concentrate on my homework. I couldn't concentrate on anything. I thought of writing to Charlotte, but even that didn't sound like fun—especially after her last letter. Our lives felt like two train tracks that used to run side by side but were now moving farther and farther apart with every passing day.

I picked up *The Magician's Handbook* and opened it to the last trick: "How to Make Yourself Levitate." I started reading it. "Getting the angles right is important for this impressive trick. Stand directly in front of your audience, raise your arms slowly to the side, and you will impress them as you create the illusion of lifting yourself off the ground."

I dropped the book back down on the floor. What was the point? This whole thing was an illusion. Imagining I could change my life and become someone really happy and popular was an illusion. Imagining my parents were better than before was an illusion.

They'd just told me they weren't even coming to the talent show tomorrow night. Dad was playing squash with his boss, for a change. And Mom had a night out with the staff at work. Nice to know where I came in their priorities. Not that I wanted them to be there, anyway. The fewer people to see me stand mute, helpless, and terrified onstage in front of the entire school, the better.

I looked around my room, wondering if I could perhaps hide in here forever. My eyes fell on the daisy in the eggcup. More than half of its petals had fallen off now. It didn't make any difference how many times I filled the water; its days were numbered — just like Daisy's — and there wasn't a single thing I could do about it.

*　*　*

Wednesday night seemed to come faster than I could have blinked. Why hadn't I just walked out of school at the end of classes and not come back this evening? Why on *earth* hadn't I done that? What was I doing here? How stupid could a person get?

The fact that I was standing there waiting for the talent show to begin — and my life as I knew it to end — was yet more proof that no matter what I pretended was happening because of my wishes, nothing had really changed. *I* hadn't changed. I was still that same scared person who never broke rules, who didn't like to let people down, who felt she had to show up just because she'd put her name on a stupid list.

Which meant I was now standing backstage in the school hall, waiting to be told my place in the lineup.

The only consolation was that at least Trisha had missed last night's shooting star. I only knew because I'd seen her at a computer in the library at lunchtime. I didn't want her to see me watching, so I sent Beth and Lauren in to find out what she was doing. She saw them coming and switched the page she was working on as soon as they came over, but not before Beth had caught a glimpse of it. She was on the Internet, and the web page had a picture of the constellations and a list of dates. She was still trying to find out the times of the shooting stars — which meant at least she hadn't made her wish yet.

There'd be another shooting star before too long. I just had to pray that she wouldn't find out when it was, or it might turn out that my problems had only just started.

"Philippa, you're last to go." Mr. Holmes, one of the teachers organizing the show, was in front of me with a clipboard. "Is that OK with you?"

It wasn't OK at all. I wanted to just get it over with, and then I could get on with running away and hiding in a cave for the rest of my life.

"That's fine," I said.

Mr. Holmes patted my arm and moved away.

"Hi, Phil." A couple of third-grade girls came up behind me. "We think you're so cool," one of them said.

"We just can't wait to see your performance," her friend added. They were both beaming at me as though they'd just found themselves in front of an

A-list superstar. I half expected one of them to ask for my autograph.

I tried to smile back at them. "Thanks," I said. My throat felt like cement, all glued up and tight. Backstage, more of the performers were hanging around, nervous and excited about the show. Without exception, when they saw me, their faces broke into wide grins. Some of them waved; some said hi; some looked too shy to talk to someone as popular as me. I felt lonelier than I'd ever felt in my life. I felt like I might be sick.

And where was Daisy?

I went to see her in the morning before I left for school. She looked terrible. She was lying on her rug, pale and weak and tired. "I'm not coming to school," she'd said. "I need to save my energy."

All day, I'd prayed that she was all right. I ran straight back to the tree house as soon as I got home—but she wasn't there. That was another thing clogging up my throat and my nerves. What had happened to her? Had her life cycle run out? Was that it? Was I ever going to see her again?

I couldn't think about it. I couldn't afford to. I had to think about this awful, horrible, stupid talent show and how I was going to get through it in one piece.

"There you are."

I whirled around to see Trisha.

"What are you doing backstage?" I asked. "You're not even in the show."

She was holding the wish voucher in her hand, waving it in front of me. "Just wanted to share the good news," she said, an evil grin spreading across her face.

"What good news?" I asked through gritted teeth, as if Trisha Miles were likely to share any good news with *me*.

"I found out when the next shooting star is. And I only have a couple of days to wait."

"Really?" I said, desperately trying to sound as if I didn't care. "So what will you wish for?"

"Well, that's for me to know and you to find out," Trisha said. "But I'll give you a clue—I won't be wishing for anything nice to happen to *you*!" She turned her back on me, laughing as she started to walk off.

As she moved away from me, for the first time since I'd set eyes on the wish vouchers, I suddenly realized something I would never have imagined could be true. I didn't need them!

If my life hadn't been working as it was, it was up to *me* to change it. It was up to me to recognize that I *could* change it. I didn't need wishes that changed everyone else's reality! How could that change *my* life? All it changed was the way others saw me, and even that wasn't real. I didn't want people to like me just because some stupid wish said they had to. Everyone in the school waving and smiling at me and wanting to change their hairstyle so it was like mine, just because I'd tricked them into it. How did that make my life better?

With the first genuine feeling of happiness I'd felt for days, I knew I'd discovered something important. I'd been busy trying to change all these things on the outside, when what mattered was what was on the inside. If I really wanted change, it had to come from inside me.

And tonight was when that had to happen.

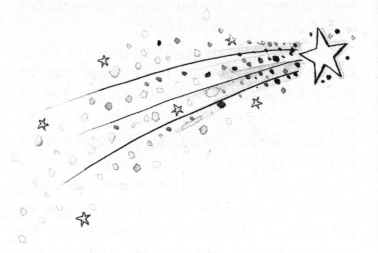

I waited for Ray. I would have paced around the glade, but I didn't have the energy. Instead I sat on the ground and waited.

Come on, come on. Please get here soon! I looked at my MagiCell for the hundredth time to see if there was a reply. I'd sent my message over an hour ago, requesting an emergency meeting. *Come on!* Soon it would be too late!

A raindrop fell on my head. Then another. Despite the sunny evening, the drops started to fall all around me. Not many, not heavily. Just enough for . . .

A rainbow.

It started off faintly, the colors all blurring into one another. Then it thinned and sharpened, reaching from the heaviest cloud in the sky, right down into the glade.

I stood up, my knees almost giving out. Rainbows were the absolute top level of ATC. Even more senior than the sun rays. I *couldn't* mess this up.

"FGRainbow9254 at your service. How can I help you?" the rainbow said in a soft voice.

I'd never met FGRainbow9254 before, but I'd heard of her. She was known for being one of the fairest of the top-level fairy godmothers, but also one of the sternest.

I took a breath. This was my last chance to back out of my plan.

I thought of Philippa, about to go onstage. I thought about what she'd told me, about what had happened all those years ago, her biggest fears. I tried to imagine how she'd be feeling right now—and I knew I couldn't back out.

"I've done something really stupid," I began.

The rainbow dipped a nod. "Go on," she said. "Tell me what you've done."

So I did. I told her all about how I'd been so angry with Philippa at the start, how I'd wanted to get the assignment over as quickly as I could, how we'd had that horrible argument and the terrible things I'd said to Trisha in the cafeteria. Then I told her how I'd felt ever since then. How

I wanted to do anything I could to show Philippa I cared. How much I wanted to help her improve her life.

The rainbow listened silently as I poured out my story.

"And then I really messed up," I said. "I lost the third wish."

"You lost it? How did you do that?"

"I wasn't careful enough. It was stolen."

"Do you know who stole it?"

I nodded. "Someone who doesn't deserve it at all. Philippa deserved her three wishes, and she still does."

I wiped a raindrop off my cheek. But it wasn't a raindrop. It wasn't even raining anymore. The drop was soon joined by another, running down my face into my mouth. Salty drops. Tears. "Please, give me a chance to help her."

"Daisy, you have had your chance to help her. You lost the final wish," the rainbow said. "Do you know there are consequences for this kind of error?"

"I know. That's why I didn't want to tell you at first. But I don't care now. You can do what you want with me. Put me on traffic duty for a year. I don't care—just please, let me help Philippa."

The rainbow stood still, piercing the glade with her bright silence. "What do you want me to do?" she said after a while.

"Trisha will never give the wish back. She'll probably

use it to do something horrible. And meanwhile, Philippa's about to perform in front of the whole school. It's her biggest fear. I promised I would help her. I promised I'd make it OK, and I *can't* let her down."

"So what do you suggest?"

"I want you to cancel Trisha's wish so she can never use it, and give me a replacement wish for Philippa, one that she can use right away." I held my breath while I waited for a reply. *"Please,"* I added.

The rainbow dipped and blurred, red blurring into orange, orange blurring into yellow, the colors dancing in front of me through my tears.

"I know I'm asking too much," I added. "I know I'll be punished. But right now, I don't care. Please do whatever you have to do to me, but just do this for her."

As I finished speaking, the rainbow expanded to fill the whole glade, surrounding me, filling me with warmth. Inside it FGRainbow9254 smiled broadly.

"How can you smile at a time like this?" I gasped.

She continued to smile. "Daisy, I was one of the few who said you were ready," she said. "Thank you for proving me right."

"Right about what? What have I done?" I asked. I didn't want to talk about me and what I could do! I wanted to talk about Philippa!

"You've passed your task, Daisy. Compassion. You've shown you can care. And I knew you could. I knew we were right to give you this task."

I didn't really understand what she was talking about— and to be honest, I wasn't really interested. All I knew was that I desperately wanted her to tell me they would do what I was asking. I'd worry about the consequences another time.

"Yes, Daisy. We will help," she added simply.

A moment later, something emerged from inside the rainbow. A new wish voucher! They'd agreed to my request! I could help Philippa!

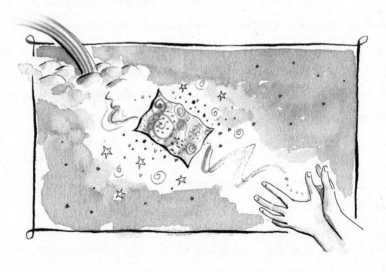

"She can use it any time. No need for shooting stars with this one. And Trisha's wish will be canceled immediately."

"Oh, thank you," I cried. "Thank you!"

"Hurry up now, but remember your life cycle," FGRainbow9254 whispered as she began to break up and fade. "You haven't got long."

"Thank you so much," I said again. Then I used all the energy I could gather to get myself out of there and back to school.

Two more acts, and then it was my turn. By now, my legs should have been turning to jelly. My insides should have been turning to mush, my heart should have been racing like a train out of control. Instead, I felt calmer than I'd felt in weeks. There was no need to be nervous. The past was the past. I was different now.

The only thing that bothered me was the fact that I would never really know what people thought of my magic tricks. Because of my silly wish, everyone would probably spend the rest of the week telling me how fantastic I was — but it would only be because they'd been brainwashed into thinking that everything I did was amazing!

And the fact that my parents weren't here. I ached from how much I wanted my old parents back.

Trisha was still around. I saw her in the wings on the other side of the auditorium, waving the wish voucher at me and smiling and looking point-edly at the clock. Let her. Let her do whatever she wanted. She wasn't going to get to me.

"Philippa!"

I turned to see who was calling me.

Daisy! She burst through the back curtains just as the act before me went onstage. Danny Treldwin, second-grader, was doing a series of dances. I was next.

"Daisy!" I breathed. "You made it!"

She looked around to check that no one was watching us. "I got you this!" she said, panting and breathless. She held something out to me. Something that sparkled and shone and sent all the colors of the rainbow whispering around the hall. "It's another wish," she said, handing me the voucher.

"But how come? Where did you get it?" I asked, taking the wish voucher from her.

"I got them to give me another one. I pleaded with them." She laughed. Her laugh turned quickly to a hacking cough, and she reached into her bag for some water.

"Daisy, are you OK?" She looked terrible. Her eyes were sunken dark holes in her face. Her hair was matted and so thin you could see her scalp.

"I'm fine," she gasped. "Just use the wish. You can have the confidence now."

"But the shooting star?"

"It doesn't matter. You can use it anytime. It's an Emergency Wish Voucher. Use it — it's yours!"

I looked down at the voucher in my hand. I had another chance at my final wish. I could use it just as we'd said. As I stood in the dark hall, I could hear the music change for Danny's final dance.

I stepped to the side, peering around the curtain at the audience. A few more minutes and it would be me on that stage, all those eyes on me.

My stomach turned over. I held the voucher out

and was about to make my wish to banish away
the fear.

"Well, well, well."

Trisha.

"What do you want?" I asked coldly.

"I just wondered if you'd like to know what I'm
going to wish for."

As I looked at her face, contorted with meanness
and spite, I felt something change inside me. The
fear in my gut was replaced with anger. "I don't
care," I said slowly. "I don't care what you wish

for. I don't care what you do — in fact I don't care about anything to do with you!"

Trisha stared at me, for once shocked and speechless. As we held each other's eyes, I realized how true my words were, how she couldn't harm me anymore.

"You see," I went on, my voice calm and measured, "I don't care about people who only get their kicks from making other people's lives worse. I don't care what you do with the wish because whatever it is, it won't be real. I won't let anything you do affect me. You're welcome to the wish voucher." I smiled at Trisha. "In fact, if you think that the wish can improve your life, then I feel sorry for you." As I spoke, everything I'd ever felt toward her — the jealousy, the anger, the humiliation — everything she'd ever done to me turned into one thing. Pity.

Trisha didn't say anything. She was still looking at me with a strange expression on her face. Disbelief, I think it was. That was probably the first time anyone had stood up to her like that. It was certainly the first time I'd stood up to her — and it felt good!

"Oh, and by the way, Trisha," Daisy said, "your

wish voucher has been canceled. You can't use it anyway."

"*What?*" Trisha reached into her pocket for her voucher — but when she pulled her hand out, it was full of what looked like shredded paper. It fell through her fingers, dissolving and floating away like a handful of ash. "What have you done with it?" she seethed.

Daisy shrugged. "I guess some things are more powerful than nastiness and spite," she said.

Smiling broadly, I turned back to Daisy as Danny's last song drew to a close. "Can I really use this now?"

She nodded.

"And I can wish for anything I want?"

"Anything." The song ended. Glimpsing around the curtain, I saw Danny take a bow as the audience burst into applause.

This was it. My one chance to wish for all the confidence I'd never had, my chance to undo the humiliation from all those years ago, my chance to seal the popularity I'd begun to have.

I looked again at Trisha's stunned face, and I knew exactly what to wish for.

The clapping was starting to die down.

"Hurry," Daisy said.

"OK." I took a deep breath. "Here goes. I wish . . ." I glanced at Daisy. She nodded for me to continue.

"I wish," I started again. I glanced at Trisha, who was watching to see what I was going to say. The clapping had finished. Mr. Holmes was onstage introducing me. I had a minute. I knew exactly what I wanted.

I spoke loud and clear. "I wish that I could undo my previous wishes." Just the chance to be myself again. I wanted it more than anything.

Daisy gawped at me. Trisha's mouth was so wide open that I could see her tonsils.

"I don't want to be the most popular girl in the school," I went on. "I just want to be me. I want people to either like me or not, but for it to be because of me, because of who I am. And I want my parents back. My crazy, nutty, embarrassing, wonderful, amazing parents."

I glanced again at Daisy. She was smiling now. Even Trisha's face had changed. I saw something new in her eyes. What was it — respect? I couldn't tell. I didn't care. What mattered most was how *I* felt about myself.

"You're sure?" Daisy asked.

Before I had a chance to reply, Mr. Holmes came offstage. "You're on," he said with a wink. I picked up the box beside me with all the objects I needed for my magic show and headed for the stage.

I paused in the wings to look back at Daisy. Holding out the voucher in my palm, I said, "I'm sure. That's my wish. Undo it all!"

With that, the voucher flew from my hand. Floating above my head, it burst into a flame of color, filling the air with swirling, whirling rainbows. Among the colors, I walked onto the stage and took a bow.

The audience looked back at me from the darkness, hundreds of pairs of shocked eyes. They must have thought the colors were my first trick! As I scanned the rows of faces, I could already tell that no one was looking at me with the expression they'd had for the last few days — that I was the most fantastic person they'd ever met, without having any reason to feel that way. It was all up to me to make them feel that way. If I did, great! But if I didn't, well, that was fine, too.

I was about to start my first trick when there was

a disturbance at the back of the hall. People were turning in their seats to see what was happening as the doors opened and a man and a woman burst through, apologizing as they searched the rows of seats for somewhere to sit down.

Mom and Dad!

Dad's hair bounced uncontrollably as they shuffled along a row of seats. Mom was wearing her torn old MEAT IS MURDER T-shirt. For a moment, the pair of them attracted more attention than me, and they weren't even performing! In the old days, I would have died right then and there, on the stage in front of the whole school. I'd have wondered how on earth they could embarrass me like that; I'd have wanted to run away and never show my face in public again.

Instead, I had never felt happier to see anyone in my whole life.

"Sorry we're late," Dad mouthed at me. And then they settled into their seats and the auditorium gradually fell into an expectant hush.

"Before I start my show, I'll need a couple of volunteers," I began. I looked down at Mom and Dad. "Maybe you could help me."

As my parents joined me onstage, I couldn't suppress a smile. They smiled back. I wanted to throw my arms around them — but that could wait. There was magic to be done.

"For my first trick, I am going to show you how to make your parents' money disappear before their eyes."

A ripple of laughter spread through the audience. I turned to Dad. "Sir, do you have a five-dollar bill on you?"

Dad handed me a five. With a flourish, I took it from him and began my first trick.

I'd done it. I'd finished my magic show. The audience had been on their feet cheering and clapping and whistling for the last five minutes and weren't showing any signs of stopping yet. I couldn't stop smiling.

"Ladies and gentlemen, the star of tonight's talent show and winner of a vacation for herself and her family, Miss Philippa Fisher!" Mr. Holmes raised my hand in the air as the audience erupted again.

Surely he was joking. I turned to look at him, and

he handed me the envelope with the prize vacation voucher in it. I'd won the talent show! I'd really won it. Me, Philippa Fisher!

The hall was filled with smiling faces — all looking at me! And it wasn't because they'd been fooled into believing I was popular. It was all totally, one-hundred percent, wonderfully, fantastically real! Everyone thought I was great — because of what I'd done. Because of my talent. Because of me.

I had to find Daisy.

As soon as the clapping died down, I ran backstage. All the other acts were there, standing around chatting together. "Philippa, you were awesome!" said a girl who'd done a mime routine. Her friends nodded their agreement.

I looked into their faces. All I could see in them was genuine approval of me and my act, not some blind hero-worship because of a wish. "Thanks," I said gratefully. "You have no idea what that means to me." They really didn't.

I looked around. "Have you seen Daisy?"

"Sorry." They shook their heads.

I ran all around the hall. "Daisy!" I called, opening doors and calling out to her everywhere. Nothing. Where was she?

As I made my way back to the main hall, I noticed a side door that was hardly ever used. It was open. Out in the yard, I saw her by a bench.

"Daisy!" I called.

She could hardly stand up. "I just needed some air," she said, her voice rasping and hoarse. Leaning on the bench for support, she smiled weakly at me. "You did it."

"*We* did it," I corrected her. "I'd never have managed it without you."

Daisy smiled feebly. "You did it, Philippa. You stood up to Trisha; you did the show. You won everyone over. You. Remember that."

"OK." I nodded. "I will."

"Good." Daisy tried to smile again, but even that looked like too much effort. Her face was gray, her eyes tiny black dots.

"Daisy," I said, my voice cracking almost as much as hers. "What's happening to you?"

"I've got to leave now," she said. She had her MagiCell in her hand. "I've only got a couple of minutes left."

A couple of minutes? She was really leaving me now? But she couldn't! "Don't go!" I urged. "Can't you ask for longer?"

She shook her head. "The life cycle's nearly finished."

"But I want to thank you."

Daisy weakly raised a hand. "Hey, I thought we'd established that you're the one who achieved this. You don't need to thank me. I messed it all up. It was you who did it."

I shook my head. "Not for the wishes," I said.

"What, then?"

I paused as I felt my cheeks heat up. "For being my best friend," I said.

It was only then that I realized it was true. I mean, Charlotte would always be my best friend—but things had changed. It would never be exactly as it had been—and neither would I! And anyway, who said you could only have one best friend?

Daisy's smile was so wide, it even managed to brighten her face up for just a second.

"Thank *you*," she said.

"What for?"

"For teaching me what it's like to *be* a real friend."

"Hey, it was easy," I said with a laugh. We both knew it had been anything but easy!

"I'll never forget you," I said, reaching out to

give her a hug. Her frail body sagged against me for a couple of seconds.

"I have to go now," she said, pulling away. Then she pressed a few buttons on her MagiCell. "Remember: you did it on your own," she said. "You can do anything!"

And then a sudden mist swept toward us. It picked up leaves and dust along the ground, whipping across my eyes and blinding me for a moment as it swirled across the playground.

When it had passed, Daisy was gone.

I sat on the bench, looking at the playground — emptier and darker than ever before.

"Hey, there you are!" Mom and Dad rounded the corner. Dad bounded over to me and threw his jacket over the arm of the bench as he lifted me off the ground in the biggest hug ever. I'd missed those hugs so much!

Mom was behind him. "We're so proud of you!" She beamed, kissing my cheeks. "Hey, you're crying," she said. "What's up?"

"Oh, it's nothing," I said. "Just happy that you made it."

"Of course we made it! We wouldn't have missed

it for the world!" Dad said. Digging Mom in the ribs to tickle her, he added, "It was your mother's fault. She had to drive to some girl's house to deliver a fairy costume from the shop."

Mom laughed. "It was so sweet," she said. "This little girl was absolutely convinced she would meet a real, live fairy as long as she wore the costume. So cute, believing in fairies. Wouldn't it be wonderful if they really existed?"

"Yeah," I said, looking up at the mist still swirling in a spiral toward the clouds as Mom and Dad each wrapped an arm around me. "It would be."

"Come on, then, let's go home," Dad said, grabbing his jacket. Then he stopped and bent down again. "Hey, look at this." He picked something up from the bench. Turning back to us, he said, "How did that get here? These don't grow on the playground."

Dad held out his hand and I peered into his palm. A daisy.

"It's beautiful," Mom said. "I've never seen one so perfect. Look at those petals, so shiny. And look at its yellow face. It almost looks as though it's smiling."

"It is," I said, smiling back at it. I could have sworn it shone even brighter then.

"Here." Dad handed it to me. "You have it. As a reminder of a wonderful evening."

I took the daisy from him, placing it carefully in my pocket and knowing it was a reminder of so much more than that.

Then Mom and Dad each threw an arm around me again and we ambled out of the playground together, all talking nonstop about the magic tricks I'd done, about the ones they liked best, the ones I'd yet to learn, the new ones I'd learned from *The Magician's Handbook* that had fooled even Dad. Others were coming out of the auditorium, crossing the playground. And I was walking across it, arm in arm with my parents!

"Hey, I'm doing a party this Saturday," Dad said. "Want to help me out?"

I paused for a moment. Could I? After all these years? Had I really managed to put it all behind me? Then I remembered what Daisy said as she'd left. *You can do anything.*

She was right; I'd proved it tonight. It didn't matter what anyone else thought. From now on,

I was going to be me. I didn't need false parents, I didn't need false friends, and I didn't need to run away from anything or anyone. I could do anything.

I turned to Dad, linking my arm more closely in his. "Of course," I said with a smile. "I'd love to."

ATC

The fairy stood in front of FGCloud3679 and FGRainbow9254.

"You did a good job," the white light of the cloud said to her. "You made your client happy—and you passed your extra task. You have developed a level of compassion that enables you to move on to higher levels now."

"Thank you," the fairy replied with a smile. "But I did get to work with the best person in the world!"

The cloud smiled back, bunching up and bouncing into a new shape. "I believe she may feel the same way about you, too, Daisy."

The fairy's smile broadened even more.

"You will be promoted into a higher life cycle for your next assignment," the rainbow said. "Now, come toward me."

The fairy walked into the rainbow, the sides of her body shimmering and dissolving until she disappeared altogether.

The rainbow brightened, glistening its full arc in colors so bright that the humans who saw it would talk about it for days afterward.

And a little while later, somewhere down on earth, a beautiful butterfly slowly edged out of its cocoon as it came to life and awaited further instructions.

This book made it all the way into your hands with a tiny bit of fairy magic and a lot of help from some very special people. Huge thanks are due to the following:

Linda Chapman, for saying exactly the right things at exactly the right time. This book would not be here without her.

Jane Cooper (Pink Bag Lady) and Andy Bennett, for helping to kick-start my story over an early morning cuppa in a tree house.

My sister, Caroline Kessler, for allowing me to spend a month working in a caravan in Anglesey surrounded by millions of children.

My agent, Catherine Clarke, for being patient and kind and taking me seriously when I said I couldn't do this writing lark anymore, and for being just as patient and also very happy when I realized I could.

My editor, Judith Elliot, for being so clever, sensitive, and understanding, for always telling me when I've got it wrong, and best of all for telling me when I get it right.

Mom, for sitting up in bed helping me sort out lots of niggles along the way — and even finding a few more once I thought I was done.

Dad — proofreader extraordinaire!

Peter B., for coming up with a solution without me ever having even told him the problem.

And Lee Weatherly, for being a great writing buddy, even when she has fairies of her own to think about.

Philippa Fisher is lonely —
she misses her fairy godsister, Daisy.

But when Daisy breaks the rules to visit
Philippa and her new friend on vacation,
things begin to go horribly wrong. . . .

Available in hardcover, paperback, and audio and as an e-book